fall for anything

Also by Courtney Summers

Some Girls Are

Cracked Up to Be

fall for anything

courtney summers

St. Martin's Griffin   New York

FALL FOR ANYTHING. Copyright © 2010 by Courtney Summers. All rights reserved.
Printed in the United States of America. For information,
address St. Martin's Press, 175 Fifth Avenue, New York, N.Y. 10010.

www.stmartins.com

ISBN 978-0-312-65673-7

10 9 8 7 6 5 4 3 2

This book is for:

My family

Sara Goodman

Emily Hainsworth

Amy Tipton

&

(always)

Lori Thibert

acknowledgments

I am more grateful to Amy Tipton and Sara Goodman than I can say. They are tireless advocates of my work, they guide my writing, they challenge me and inspire me to do better, and they also put up with a lot. They've made each of my books possible and it's an honor to work with them. They have all my admiration and respect.

All my thanks to the wonderful folks at St. Martin's Press, particularly Katy Hershberger, for everything they do on behalf of me and my books. I appreciate it tremendously.

I have a great family and can't imagine doing any part of this without them, which is why this book is dedicated to them! They are: Susan. David. Megan. Jarrad. Marion. Ken. Lucy. Bob. Damon. All my love and thanks.

Lori Thibert and Emily Hainsworth's support, encouragement, and endless listening saved my life this time around. Needless to say, I owe them a lot. They are both amazing, but not just because of that. I'm president of the Canadian chapter of their respective fan clubs.

Whitney Crispell, Kim Hutt, Baz Ramos, and Samantha Seals

are strong, hilarious, passionate, amazing, incredible women and their friendship keeps me going. I am developing a plan where I somehow become all four of them when I grow up. Brilliant and sparkly!

An ocean of thanks to these people: Emily. Linda. Scott. Susan. Tiffany. Victoria. (Hi, Team!) Adele. Allie. Annika and Will. Brian. Briony. Carolyn. Daisy. Damon. Jessica. Kelvin. Nova. Tristan. Veronique.

I have to mention Lori one more time. There are about five thousand reasons she winds up in the dedication of every novel I've written and I regret not having the space here to list them all. She is amazing and I aspire to her levels of generosity, patience, kindness, and talent. I'm lucky to know her and to call her a friend. Thank you, Lori.

The publication of my novels has connected me to some of the most incredible readers, writers, and bloggers. Their love of and enthusiasm for young adult literature constantly awes me. I can't thank them enough for the time and support they have given to me and to my books.

There are always so many people to thank and not enough space to do it! Much gratitude and love to all of my family and friends.

fall for anything

M y hands are dying.
    I keep trying to explain it to Milo, but he just looks at me like I'm crazy.

"They don't feel warm—they haven't." I squeeze the tips of my fingers as hard as I can, which hurts. "They're not numb, though . . ."

"Maybe you have that . . . Raynaud's disease," he says. He takes my right hand and studies my fingers. They seem healthy, pink. He shakes his head. "They're not blue."

"But they're cold."

"They feel warm to me."

"They feel cold," I insist.

"Okay, Eddie," he says. "They're cold."

I jerk my hands from his and then I rub them together. Friction. Heat. Milo can say what he wants; they're freezing. It's the hottest summer Branford has seen in something like ten years, but I haven't been able to get my hands to warm up since it happened.

I hold them up again. They don't even look like my hands anymore. They don't even look like anything that could belong to me, even though they're clearly attached.

"They're different," I tell him.

"Would you please put your hands down?" he asks. "Jesus."

My hands have changed. I catch Milo looking at them sometimes, and I see it on his face that they're different, no matter what he's saying now.

We're at the park, sitting on the picnic tables, watching a summer world go by. Kids play in the fountain with their parents. Pant legs are rolled up and big hands are holding on to tiny hands, keeping them steady against the rush of water. The smell of burgers and fries is in the air; food. It reminds me the fridge at home is empty and I have to go grocery shopping today or my mom and I will starve. I don't even know how long the fridge has been that empty, but I noticed it today.

"What's in your fridge?" I ask Milo.

"Doesn't matter," he says. "My mom isn't home."

We're stuck between my house and his lately. He hasn't been allowed to have girls at his place unsupervised since he hit puberty and I don't like hanging out at my place now.

It's too depressing.

"That's not why I asked. I have to go grocery shopping and I don't know what to get . . ." I rest my chin in my hands. "And I really don't want to do it."

He hops off the picnic table. "Let's just get it over with, okay?"

We make our way out of the park and go to the grocery store. I've barely stepped through the automatic doors when I decide it is The Saddest Place on Earth.

Everyone just looks *sad*.

We end up in produce. I give myself a headache over the kind of math you have to use to buy food, which you need to live. I don't even know what I want or what we need or how much I should be spending or what's reasonable to spend. EVERYTHING HERE IS A STEAL, if I believe the signs, but there are two grocery stores in Branford, so I don't know.

"It's not hard," Milo says, but even he sounds kind of unsure.

It *is* hard. I've never done this before.

I never had to.

We head to the frozen foods and I start shoving TV dinners into my cart and then I go to the dairy aisle and get cheese and bread because it seems less hopeless than TV dinners. And then I stand there, lost. What's next? This is what grown-ups do.

It's such a waste of time.

"Hey," Milo says. "You here?"

"I'm here," I say. I think.

I head back to the freezers and grab some frozen vegetables. I read somewhere they're better for you than fresh because they were picked at a perfect moment in time and frozen in it. Fresh vegetables aren't really fresh because as soon as they're out of the ground and on their way to the grocery store, the best parts of them have already started to fade away.

"I should get . . ."

I trail off and turn in the aisle, trying to ignore the sad faces shuffling past, and then I grab some ginger ale. Ginger ale is usually only for when we're sick and I know we're not technically sick, but every time I'm at home, I feel like I could puke so that must be close enough.

When we step inside my house, all the lights are off.

It wouldn't be a big deal since it's summer and it's the middle of the day, but all the curtains are drawn too. It's like some kind of permanent dusk or twilight here now—those two points in twenty-four hours where it's too early or too late to do anything. I'm discovering those moments feel like they go on forever. Milo reaches for the first light switch he sees, but I stop him and bring my finger to my lips. I keep it there until I hear it.

That voice.

"You'd feel *so* much better if you had one room that was neat and clean . . ."

Enemy presence confirmed.

Now I just have to figure out how to sneak the groceries into the fridge and leave again before *she* notices I'm here.

"—get Eddie to clean the living room up, start your day there every morning. Have your tea, center yourself, and let it motivate you into creating a new routine. You can't stagnate, Robyn. I was talking to Kevin about it. You have to *force* yourself to *adjust*, basically . . ."

Beth.

I back into Milo because all her voice makes me want to do is run, but our grocery bags rustle against each other, and just like that, it's over for both of us.

"Eddie?" Beth's voice is glass-edge sharp and goes straight up my spine. Milo rubs my shoulder with his free hand. "Eddie? Is that you?"

I turn on the light. "It's me . . ."

We step into the kitchen. Beth is there, her arms crossed. Behind her, I glimpse my mother. She's at the table, wrapped up in Dad's old housecoat.

"Where have you been?" Beth asks. She nods at the bags. "What are those?"

Beth has been my mother's best friend since way before I was born. Beth is what happens to mean girls after they graduate high school. Beth is what happens to mean girls after they graduate high school and turn forty. Beth is what happens to mean girls after they graduate high school, turn forty, and develop *gerontophobia* and *thanatophobia*, which means she's unnaturally afraid of getting older and dying, which would be sad if her endless Botox injections and vitamin-popping and paranoid trips to the doctor weren't so mockable. She's always hated me. She wishes Mom and Dad never got married or had a kid because my existence just reminds her of how old she's getting.

Beth has spent every waking hour trying to emotionally bleach this place out and turn it back the way it was, but it will never be the way it was.

Beth is driving me fucking crazy.

"They're groceries," I tell her. She holds out her hands and I give the bags over. Milo does the same. "The fridge was empty."

Mom wordlessly opens her arms and gestures me forward. My heart inches up my throat and I go to her, burying my face in the housecoat. It's starting to smell less and less like him and more like her. She grips me tightly.

"Leave a note," she whispers. Her voice is crackly. "Next time you leave the house, leave a note, okay?"

I nod and she lets me go. I feel Milo watching us. Sometimes I hate that he does. I know he can't help being in front of it, but he doesn't have to look.

Beth riffles through my purchases. "These will have to be returned. You can't have this in the house. It's not healthy. *TV* dinners, Eddie? Processed food is like *eating* death—"

"But the fridge was empty—"

"I know. Your mother called me."

Beth opens the fridge with a flourish, and where once was nothing, now is everything, and everything is lame. The crisper is full of bright colors; vegetables. Cartons of yogurt line the bottom shelf, and from here I can see she's organized them alphabetically by flavor. Cottage cheese. Hummus. She goes into the cupboards, opens them, and I spot boxes of couscous and tabouleh and dried beans and I completely lose interest in food forever.

She closes the doors and stares at me accusingly.

"How did you let it get down to *nothing*?" She sets my bags on the floor in front of me. "Take these back. We don't need them."

"But the ginger ale—"

"Take them back," she repeats firmly. "And by the way, your mother and I were talking. We thought you could clean up the living room—to give her a space where she can create a new routine. Begin the process of starting over. I was talking to Kevin and Kevin said—"

"Kevin as in Kevin your *esthetician*?"

Milo snorts and Beth turns red. She takes a *deep, cleansing breath*—at least that's what she calls them, but I don't think deep, cleansing breaths go in and out through the narrow spaces between clenched teeth—and after a long moment, she smiles very, very sweetly, which is what she always does before she spews her sugared venom at me.

"I'm just curious—what about that idea sounds unreasonable

to you?" She crosses her arms. "Please tell me, Eddie. Let's have a nice talk about this."

"Can't." I pick up the grocery bags, ginger ale and all. "I have to take these back."

I glance at Mom again, looking for some kind of reaction. She hates when I fight with Beth, usually implores us both to stop, but she's quiet, her hands clutching her housecoat closed.

She's staring at the wall, where there is a photograph of my father.

In the photo, he's laughing.

Milo and I have this drinking game about Beth: every time she annoys me, we drink.

She annoys me a lot.

"So what do you think Elizabeth Bathory is doing right now?" I ask.

"I don't know," Milo says.

I tilt my face toward the sun. Beth stays out of the sun as much as possible. She doesn't want wrinkles or cancer, but she's a walking spray-on tan because she doesn't want to look old either. For her next birthday, I'm going to break into her house and fill it with clocks.

I take a swig from Milo's flask and hand it back to him. He screws the top back on. He inherited the flask from his grandfather and stole the liquor from his mom. The circle of life.

Or something.

"Do you think she's gone yet?"

"Beth?" he asks. I nod and he laughs. "No. She's going to stay there until you get back so she can give you the last word."

"I fucking hate her."

"I know you do."

We're sprawled out on the dry, yellow grass next to Ford River, which curls through Branford. This summer is so dry, the water barely trickles by the stones that peak far past its surface. It's painfully low. You could walk across it and never get your feet wet.

"Watch this," I say, getting up. "I mean, watch me."

"Twist my arm."

I give Milo a look. He returns a lazy smile. I stand, slip out of my sandals, and edge my way down to the bank. I place one bare foot on a large, sturdy rock and move to the next closest rock easily, even though it's smaller. I hop to the next and the next and then I'm in the middle of the river, which seems far enough. I face Milo and he claps.

"Take that show on the road," he calls.

I bow and make my way back to him. I settle on the ground and ease my head against his outstretched shins, like they're a pillow. I stare at the sky. It's clear, no clouds or anything. Just the sun, until it burns out billions of years from now.

"What are you thinking?" Milo asks. I hold up my hands. I don't even say anything and he goes, "Eddie, please don't make me feel up your hands again."

"Why?"

"Because I won't."

"I bet if I asked, you would."

"Probably."

Milo would do almost anything for me. He's been my best friend since second grade, when a brief but weird obsession with the original *Star Trek* got him sort of ostracized at the same time all the girls in our class decided a girl named Eddie must actually really be a boy. By third grade, we weren't so outcast anymore, but we were beyond needing other people. We still are. Anyone else who happens on the both of us, they're just temps.

Like that girlfriend he had that one time.

"Tell me about that night," I say.

He shakes his head.

He would do almost anything for me.

I look back at my hands.

"They *are* dying."

He turns his head toward the water and squints, like he's caught sight of something very interesting, but it's a lie. The sun is on him and he looks like he just rolled out of bed, but he always looks like that. His longish brown hair is always messy around his head. His blue eyes always look kind of sleepy. I lower my hands.

"So, are you going to be home later tonight?" he asks.

"Later like when?"

"Like, after ten." He's leaving me soon. I can feel it. Mostly because he has a part-time job at Fuller's Gas and it's getting to be that time. "I have to go to work."

"I'm crashing early tonight," I lie.

like to make my nighttime escapes unnecessarily dramatic because it makes it easier to ignore the weight in my chest. I can briefly fool my body into believing I'm going on an *adventure*.

The adventure starts when it's late enough that everyone is asleep, usually just Mom, but sometimes Beth. Tonight Beth is staying over. I get out of bed as quietly as possible and then I open my window, fighting with it, because the house is shrinking or the window is expanding—I'm not sure—and when it's open, I crawl onto the roof, which slopes down, and make my way carefully to the very edge of it on my butt until my legs dangle over the side. It's not a long drop by any stretch of the imagination, but it feels farther standing up, so I don't.

I'm still impressed with the fact I can jump off the roof and land perfectly each time. Okay, not the first time. Definitely not the first time. I landed hard on my knee that time, but it wasn't enough to keep me from leaving. It was enough that I bled, sticky red all down my leg—but that just told me I was alive.

I jump.

It's effortless.

It is so easy.

I land. The ground is a shock against my feet, like it always is. Landing makes me dizzy. My cell phone vibrates in my back pocket. Milo. I ignore it.

I grab my bike and I get on it and I just go.

Branford is so still this late at night. Shuts down after nine o'clock. There are no cars headed anywhere and the roads are silent. Every so often I pass a house with an air-conditioner in the window and its rattling drone fills the street. When it fades, there's only the soft rush of my bike wheels on the pavement. The first night, I walked. It's too far to walk.

He walked.

come out here every night.

It's still dark out when I get back, close to morning.

I can't get inside the house like how I get out of it. I go around the back and in through the glass doors off the patio that open into my dad's old office. I sit in his old chair, at his desk. I lean my head back and close my eyes. The chair is falling apart because he wore it down, got it to fit him perfectly. He refused to throw it out and now I'm trying hard to belong to the space he left behind, but I'm awkward and small and I don't.

Sometimes, when my eyes are closed, I can convince myself I smell him: old paper and musk and something chemical. I open my eyes, expecting to see him but there's nothing.

The door creaks open.

My heart stops. I jump out of the chair fast.

Beth. She turns on the light and squints at me.

"I thought I heard someone," she says.

I don't say anything. Just wait for her to go. Of course, she doesn't. She steps inside and moves around the office slowly, taking it all in. I don't know if she's been in here since my dad died.

She pauses and studies some of the photographs he took that hang on the wall. *Leave.* I don't say it, though. It's a miracle she hasn't noticed I'm still dressed.

"Such a waste," she murmurs.

"What's a waste?" I ask.

She gestures to the photos. "To have that kind of gift . . . to have people respond to it." She pauses. "And then to just . . . stop sharing it."

My father was famous.

A long, long time ago.

Maybe famous is the wrong word. My father was an artist, and to other artists he was a star. But I only know this about my father so long after it's been true, maybe *star* is the wrong word too. When he was twenty, he went by his initials, S.R., and turned an entire city into his own personal art gallery. He spent a year pinning his photos all over city walls, shots of people close and touching everywhere, until eventually, the media noticed. It took six months for them to out him, and when they asked him why he'd done it, he said, *I want to share my work with the world.* Simple. The world was charmed.

Later, he told me it wasn't his art or his sincerity, it was just the right time. Either way, he was briefly catapulted into the kind of life I've never been able to imagine him living, but spend more and more time trying to imagine him living.

Secrets on City Walls became a book.

His work was in actual galleries, in far more places than he's ever been.

When my dad was twenty-five, some celebrity of the day announced in an interview she'd started a collection of his work and she wanted them all, every last photo, and then everyone else did too—even if they didn't, not really.

That was when my father walked away from it all.

He says—said, *said*—that's what people remember about him

most: he had the world at his fingertips and he walked away. He asked that he be forgotten, so he could give his art back to himself. Somehow, everyone found that message way less endearing.

At thirty, he moved to Branford. Branford is a good place to be forgotten.

To become a reclusive artist who never stops creating, but stops sharing.

He worked in a studio two hours away until he died.

And now he's dead.

"Oh," I say. "I thought you were talking about his suicide."

She gives me this look.

"I don't need to say that about his suicide." She points to a photograph next to his bookshelf. It's of my mom, dad. Me. Family portrait. She points to Mom and Dad and she says, "Twenty. Your mother was twenty when they eloped. He was forty-five."

"*Really?*" I ask. "Wow, Beth. I totally did not know this."

She ignores my tone. "She was only twenty-four when she had you—she was never an adult without your father, Eddie." She fixes me with one of her trademark looks of superiority. "Maybe you could remember that the next time I'm asking you to do something to make it a little easier for her, like tidying up the living room. Because when you act like that, you're not making it hard on me. You're making it hard on her."

"Good night, Beth."

She sighs, but she gets the hint. She turns off the light and leaves me in the dark. I sit back down in the chair and close my eyes, trying to conjure my father's ghost, waiting for the Seth Reeves I knew to feel close.

The Seth Reeves I knew: gentle and quiet. Giving. The man who laughed every time someone mistook him for my grandfather, which happened a lot because, at sixty-four, he looked like one. The man who killed spiders at my tearful requests and tried—and failed—to teach me to drive, danced with his wife in the kitchen and smiled . . .

That man would never get rid of himself.

So now I am looking for his death in his art.

It's the thing I know least about him.

I reach across his desk and rest my hands on the note he left, which has stayed there since we found it. I run my fingers over the paper, crumpled from Mom's grasp before she set it back and smoothed it out as much as she could, pretending it hadn't been touched or read. All it says is that he had to leave, he loves us both. My mom clutched her chest the first time she read it and I thought she was going to die and I glimpsed a future, myself alone—completely alone—and thought I would die too. But I'm still here. And he's not.

I need to know why.

Good morning, Eddie!"

I open my eyes. Beth's face is inches from my face. I can smell her perfume, something expensive and awful. Her green eyes are bright. She's either been up for ages or she was snorting lines of cocaine in the bathroom. Or both. I glance at the clock on my nightstand. I've been asleep three hours. Maybe.

"After I caught you prowling around the house last night, it got me thinking about circadian rhythms," she says, clapping her hands. "And then your mom told me you're up *very* late these days. Maybe you have a sleep disorder. I think we need to get you back on track." She sits on the edge of my bed while I briefly marvel at the fact Mom notices anything I do these days. "I was talking to Kevin—"

"God, what is he?" I grumble. "An esthetician-slash-life coach?"

"—*And* he made a really good point. We should focus on *not* doing things that exacerbate the inherent sadness of this situation and do what we can to maintain a *positive balance* as much as possible. Did you know lack of sleep is detrimental to a positive attitude? You need to make sure you get enough sleep. *And* you should exercise, get those endorphins going! Eat healthy! Come down-stairs and have breakfast!"

"No."

"But your mother would love to see you at the breakfast table. She told me so." She gets off the bed. "Positive attitude, Eddie! I'll see you in five or I'll come back for you in ten."

She leaves. I roll over and stare at the ceiling. I hate when Beth stays the night. Mom upgrades from zombie to total robot, which isn't much of an improvement because it just means she'll do any-thing Beth tells her to do. Beth tells her to get out of bed and she does it. Beth tells her to eat and she'll eat. Beth won't ask her to get out of Dad's housecoat, but she'll get Mom used to the idea, suggest it in a way that won't lead to a total breakdown, like I accidentally did the second week after he died.

But I guess easing Mom into the idea of getting out of the housecoat isn't a bad thing.

Not that it makes me hate Beth any less.

Breakfast. More *positivity* than I know what to do with. Mom dredges bite-size pieces of pancake through sticky maple syrup, but none of them actually reach her mouth. I wonder if Beth pre-cut her food. I wonder if, in the future, Beth will have to pre-chew it.

Gross.

Mom stares out the window like there's nothing more fascinat-ing than the maple tree in the front yard. Beth follows her gaze. I sip at my coffee. It's decaf.

Beth has brought decaf into this house.

"It's almost better that it's summer," Beth says thoughtfully. "Then you're not dealing with SAD on top of everything else . . ."

I choke. That's the dumbest to come out of her mouth yet. It's so dumb I start to giggle, and I shake so much I have to set my coffee down. And then I start to *really* laugh. I laugh so hard I have trou-ble breathing. Mom finally turns her gaze from the window and stares at me, but her eyes are so empty. I want to wave my hand in front of her face and say, *hello? Is anyone there? Are you hearing this?* But I can't because I can't seem to stop laughing.

And Beth looks at me like *I'm* crazy when I finally do.

"I'm *so* glad you find that amusing, Eddie," she says.

"When are you leaving?" I ask her. "Like, don't you have somewhere else to be?"

"Actually, it's funny you should say that because it turns out I'm going to be staying with you for a while," Beth says. She smiles at me, but it's not really a smile. "Maybe a month."

"What?" I turn to Mom. She's not looking at me anymore. "I'm sorry—*what?*"

"Because you need someone here," Beth tells me. "To get all the . . ." she trails off, but I know what she wanted to say. *Death.* To get all the death out. "You need someone here to bring some positive energy to this place."

"But I'm here," I say.

And then *Beth* starts laughing.

am going to explode.

I put on my shoes and leave the house half-dressed. I'm wearing shorts with a pajama top that hopefully passes for a T-shirt if no one looks closely at the cartoon sheep slumbering over the big bubble letters across the chest that say NIGHTY-NIGHT NIGHTIE.

I leave on my bike, pumping my legs hard because I'm angry and I don't know how else to work it out. I check my watch. Milo is at Fuller's right now, killing time until two, when his cousin Mark relieves him and then we can skulk around Branford with less purpose than anyone else in this dumb town.

I bike across two streets, cut through an alleyway and round the corner off the main street. Fuller's comes into view. The place is busy. One truck, three cars, a self-serve parade. The closer I get to it, the sounds, the smells, everything feels like too much. Instead of slowing down and pushing the handbrakes or even dragging my feet, I speed up, pumping my legs harder, until I can feel it in my heart. I just keep moving—

Until the back of the truck stops me.

I guess I'm not going as fast as I think I am. Maybe it only felt like my legs were matching pace with my pulse. Still, when I hit the truck, it makes this awful sound. My stomach ricochets off my spine and instead of going over the handlebars and into the truck bed, I sort of flop right over. I land on my side and my bike collapses on top of me. I close my eyes.

I don't feel so much like exploding anymore.

I mean, I think I could sleep here.

"What the *fuck* did you *do* to my *fucking truck*?!"

I open my eyes. The guy the truck belongs to stands over me. He's wearing an unbuttoned plaid shirt over one of those greasy, off-white undershirts and his arms are hairy and the knees of his jeans are so worn out it's amazing they're still attached. Roy Ackman. Farmer. Everyone knows Roy.

He came to the funeral.

He is giving me the weirdest look right now.

"Eddie Reeves?" he asks, totally bewildered. I'm the last person on earth he's expecting. Before I can say anything, the jingling of the bells over the front door to the store sound. Open. Close. Milo. I hear him before I see him.

"*Jesus*, Eddie!"

Roy lifts my bike off me. "You got a problem with my truck?"

"Why didn't you *stop*?" Milo demands, looming over me.

"Uhm . . ." I lick my lips. Milo extends his hand and I fumble to get my fingers around his. I can't figure out how to work them because when I say they're dying, I mean it. I can't hold on. It takes forever, but I finally get a grip and Milo pulls me to my feet. As soon as I'm upright, his hand is on the small of my back, like he's keeping me steady.

"I spaced out," I say. "I guess."

Milo just stares at me, but Roy's face softens like that, and I sort of hate that I'm going to get away with this for all the wrong reasons, but I think I have to let it happen because everyone in Branford knows how Roy Ackman feels about his truck.

"I'm really sorry, Roy," I add. "I didn't mean to."

"No, no," he says gruffly, waving a hand. "It's okay. I know . . ."

He looks me right in the eyes. I didn't notice how blue Roy Ackman's eyes were until this exact moment. He shoves his hands in his pockets, rocks back on his heels, and starts vomiting small-town condolences all over me.

"So, is your mom doing okay? We miss seeing her around town. If you ever want to come down, we'd love to have you for dinner. Corinne keeps meaning to call to let you know our door's always open to you . . ."

I rub my arm. "Yeah . . . thanks."

"Okay, then . . ." He keeps staring until he snaps to, remembering where he is and what he was doing before I decided to play chicken with his Chevy. He goes in his pocket for his wallet, pulls out a twenty, and hands it to Milo. "Twenty even. I'll be on my way."

Milo salutes him. "Have a good one, Roy."

We watch Roy pull out and then I grab my bike and make my way to the store, resting it against the building before pushing through the door. The air-conditioning feels good.

Milo edges in behind me.

"What the fuck was that?"

"Beth served gluten-free pancakes and decaf for breakfast. And she's moving in for like a month." I lean against the freezer full of pop and energy drinks. "You seem busy."

"Kind of."

He goes to the counter and pours two coffees, no cream and no sugar—straight up. He doubles up on the cups so we don't burn our hands because the Styrofoam gets hot and then he grabs two pepperoni sticks from the jar beside the cash register and hands me one and he never pays, but it doesn't matter because his aunt owns the place and she doesn't care. Milo is on all the surveillance tapes, eating up the food, but as long as she never has to work the register, it's totally fine.

"Sorry about Beth," he says, looking me up and down. His gaze lingers on my NIGHTY-NIGHT NIGHTIE. He doesn't say anything, which is good. I yawn. "Tired?"

"I was up late."

"Really? Because I called you last night and you didn't pick up."

"Sorry." I take a sip of the coffee, which is stupid. It burns all the way down. "Beth woke me up as soon as I got to sleep. She says I need to get my cicada rhythms back on track."

His mouth quirks. "You mean *circadian* rhythms?"

"What are you, Beth?"

A customer comes in, and then another and another. Milo stands alert behind the register and I just stay there, yawning, until he says, "Take the couch. I'll wake you when my shift ends."

I go to the backroom and flop down on the gross leather couch that has been here since time immemorial and that, despite its grossness, is actually really comfortable. I close my eyes and next thing, Milo is shaking me awake and the light coming in through the window has changed.

"Gus is here," he says.

I rub my face and follow Milo back into the store, squinting, trying to wake myself up. As soon as Milo's uncle sees me, he envelops me in this big bear hug and I can't figure out why until I realize this is the first time I've seen *him* since the funeral too. Gus doesn't usually follow one of Milo's shifts. Mark must have cancelled.

"Holding up?" He keeps his voice low.

"Yep," I say into his chest.

It takes him forever to let go, or maybe it just feels like it. I can't wait to get out of his grasp, but as soon as I am, I sort of want to be hugged again.

Gus claps Milo on the shoulder.

"So what's on the agenda for you two today? Trouble?"

"Of course," Milo says.

Of course. We leave Fuller's, making our way to the park so we can sit there and do nothing. Milo walks my bike for me, like he doesn't trust that I won't just pedal myself into the back of another truck. We don't talk. It's quiet between us lately. All the time. Sometimes I'm afraid my dad's death has stolen whatever sparked between us back in the second grade.

We never used to be this kind of quiet.

'm edging down the roof like usual when I catch myself on a nail that wasn't there before. I tear the skin of my thigh on it and I feel my blood soaking into my jeans. When I hit the ground, my cell phone rings. Milo. I forgot to set it to vibrate. The ringtone is obscenely loud against all the nighttime around me and the only way I can think to make it stop is to answer him, so I do.

"What's going on?" I ask.

"I thought you'd be asleep." He sounds surprised. "It's late."

"No. What's going on?"

I tiptoe around the house to get my bike, trying to be as quiet as possible. The reception crackles a little. I hope he doesn't know I'm outside, that he can somehow figure this out.

"Nothing . . . That truck thing today was pretty fucked up."

"I know." I walk my bike to the street slowly. "Sorry."

"No, it's fine—I mean, it's not fine. I mean, that's not why I called."

"Why did you call?"

And then I get this crazy thought that he is finally going to tell me about that night because the silence on the other end of the line is so heavy, so important.

This has to be it.

"I don't know," he says. Or maybe not. "What are you doing?"

"Nothing," I lie. "What are you doing?"

"Nothing."

Silence. And then he fakes a yawn and says, "Look, I should call it a night but I'll see you tomorrow or something, okay?"

"Okay," I say.

He hangs up.

I leave.

This place never has anything to say to me.

Beth's luggage precedes her, which is horrifying, and as soon as she steps through the door, she immediately throws herself into making the house a "more positive place."

"It's all about how you *choose* to be," she tells me as she sticks magnets with inspirational quotes all over the fridge. She also brought a few plants—ferns, mostly. I feel bad for them. No one is going to water them and they'll die. "You need more light—" She walks to the window and pulls back the blinds, giving me a look like *I'm* the one who drew them closed in the first place. "Vitamin D! Essential. Do you know how many diseases a little bit of sun can *prevent*? I have a list somewhere in my purse. . . ."

She flits out of the room before I can respond. Mom is upstairs doing I don't know what, so I guess I'm the welcoming committee. A second later, one of those Sounds of Nature CDs is filling up the entire house. We now live in a rain forest.

Beth reenters the room and notices the look on my face.

"For meditative purposes," she informs me.

I roll my eyes. "Because we meditate so much around here."

"Maybe it's time you started," she says. "Stress is a killer."

"Then I should be dead really soon, because you're stressing me out."

"Oh, Eddie." She comes over and pinches my cheek, something she used to do when I was five. I hated it then too. "I wish making *you* a more positive person was as simple as all this! You need to stop looking at me as the enemy and start looking at me as a *reprieve*."

When her back is to me, I turn my fingers into a gun and aim it directly at her head.

Fuller's is pretty empty, except for a blue Ford Taurus parked next to the store.

I don't think anything of it until I get to the door and I see who it belongs to and then I don't know what to think. Her back is to me and she's leaning over the counter talking to Milo, but I don't need to see her face to know who it is. I would recognize those legs anywhere. They're perfect and tanned. Go all the way up.

Missy Vinton.

Milo looks up from his spot behind the counter and sees me at the door. I hold up a hand and take a step back like, *forget it, I'll go,* but he shakes his head and Missy turns to see who he's staring at and when she sees me, she hurries over and opens the door.

The last time I saw Missy—before she moved during junior year—she was turning into Marilyn Monroe.

Now the transformation is complete.

Missy Vinton.

That girlfriend Milo had that one time.

"*Eddie!* Oh my God!" Missy exclaims. She throws her arms

around me and squeezes me so hard I can't breathe. "It's *so* good to see you!"

I don't know what to say. I stare at Milo over her shoulder. He's looking straight at me, but I can't read his expression.

Missy Vinton.

It took forever for him to ask her out. He never said *love* and I know it wasn't, but he wanted her so bad he had no problem telling me just how much. He was the one who pointed out the Marilyn Monroe thing (only a fleeting resemblance at the time) and he'd always make these really lame jokes about changing his name to Joe. And then, in the middle of sophomore year, at some party at Deacon Hunt's, he got drunk enough to tell her so.

And I guess she'd liked him for ages too.

They were the loneliest ten months of my life.

"Welcome back," I tell her.

"Thank you. I am so," Missy says, and then she pauses right there. Pause. I steel myself for what's coming next. "Sorry about your father, Eddie. Like, really, really sorry."

"Thank you," I say, and she finally pulls away. "Wow, Missy. This is a surprise."

"Really? I told Milo I was coming in, like, May. I'm staying the summer—with my grandparents." She turns around to look at him. "You didn't tell her?"

"No," I say before he can. "He didn't."

It's not subtle. Not the way it comes out of my mouth. And I'm sorry for the way it comes out of my mouth because I don't want to cause this kind of tension. Missy actually steps back like I'm going to bite her or freak and I want to tell her it's not her, even though it's her. But it's also *not* her. It's Milo.

It's Milo not telling me.

"Why didn't you tell me?" I try to keep my voice light.

Because Missy and Milo never really broke up. They just stopped. She moved. They didn't write. They didn't talk on the phone. I know he missed her. So maybe it wasn't a full stop between them so much as it was only a pause. Pause. Resume play.

Fantastic.

"I was going to," he says awkwardly. "But then . . . your dad . . ."

"Oh," I say. And then I laugh. I don't know why or where it comes from. Nervous laugh. Missy shifts, awkward, and even Milo looks uncomfortable and I'm already a third wheel. "Oh, right." I nod. "Right. That makes sense. Sorry." This is painful. "So I should go."

"But you just got here," he says.

"I know, but I don't want to interrupt."

"You're not—"

"I am." I take a few steps back and pull the door open. "I mean, I did."

don't come here during the day, ever.

I come at night, waiting for some piece of the puzzle to click into place, waiting to understand, and I stay until the living world presses in on me and I have to go back to it, but this is the first time since my dad died that I have nowhere else to go. Not home, where Beth is, and not at Fuller's with Milo, where Missy is. All that's left is here.

The last place my father was.

Tarver's Warehouse is old and abandoned. It didn't start out in the middle of nowhere. This used to be somewhere and it used to be something, but now it's a "notable stop" on the type of Web sites that spotlight modern-day ruins next to towns that are quickly becoming the same. It stands in the middle of an old dirt lot that has weeds growing up around it. It's condemnable.

It's floor after floor of broken windows that go so far up . . .

The warehouse looks even worse under direct sunlight. No shadows to cloak how truly run-down the place is, how dangerous. The windows seem more broken, the foundation more crumbly. Desolate. I can almost understand how someone would come here with the intention to die, but at the same time, he came here all the time before that moment, just to photograph it.

And he came back.

I set my bike on the ground and sit next to it, bringing my knees to my chest. I should think about how something inside you changes and you can decide nothing is worth living for anymore, but instead, I think about Milo and Missy. Missy is here now. For the summer. There is no good time for Missy, really, but this is the worst possible time.

Her being here feels like a bee sting.

I run my hand over the dirt and grit. Milo will call me tonight, I know it. He'll want to talk about Missy. He'll ask me if I hate her. (I don't.) I'll tell him it's fine, even though it's not, because what can either of us do about it?

I would never make him do anything about it.

I don't know how long I'm sitting in the dirt, fixating on this before I feel like I'm not alone. A chill crawls up my spine and I look up. The roof is empty. I'm too afraid to go up there, even though that's all I want to do. I want to go up there and see if there are any traces of my dad left, but just the idea makes my palms sweat and I can't breathe. I tried to, once. I got inside and tried so hard to fumble my way up to the roof in the dark, but I just couldn't do it.

I stand and brush off my jeans. There's no one on the roof, but I can't shake that feeling.

Someone's here, somewhere.

I scan the windows because something in my gut is telling me to and that's when I see it—a face coming through one of the pieces of glass, warped and distorted. I stumble back at the shock of it. I'm *not* alone. But then I blink and the face is gone.

I've seen scary movies like this before. This is that moment just before I get killed. I try to pick up my bike, but my dying hands are going out on me and it takes forever to get the thing righted, and by the time I do there's a voice behind me.

"Hey. Wait—"

It's not a voice I recognize. A boy's voice. I stop moving, but I don't turn around. His footsteps crunch across the gravel and dirt and my head is telling me to *move* but I don't.

The footsteps stop just short of me. I keep my back to them.

"I saw you from the window," the boy says. "I startled you . . . sorry."

I'm still startled. I can't make myself turn around. He sounds okay, but I'm afraid whoever he is—that he won't have a nice face. The way it came through the window made it seem creepy. But this should be the last thing that worries me. There are so many other reasons to be afraid of a strange guy hanging around an abandoned warehouse outside of town, but . . .

I face him.

I don't know what I'm expecting. Maybe not this. Maybe exactly this. A boy, kind of. Post-boy? He's definitely older than seventeen, but not twenty-five, and he has a five o'clock shadow and needs to shave. There's a camera around his neck. A Nikon. He's wearing jeans and a T-shirt, and the T-shirt he's wearing has a big white arrow pointing down, so for a second, I'm staring at his crotch when I should be staring at his face.

His face: he has a mop of dirty-blond hair and hazel eyes.

The whole time I'm studying him, he's studying me.

He takes a step back, a small smile on his mouth.

His eyes travel from my feet, up my legs, lingering on my hips, my waist, past my chest, to my eyes. A voice inside my head tells me I should go because this isn't safe because awkward moments like these can precede far more sinister things, but instead I ask, "Are you a photographer or are you just pretending?"

He brings his hands to his Nikon but he doesn't say anything. I wonder if he's a vulture. If he was somehow aware this was a place my father frequented or if more people come out here to take photographs than I ever knew about. After a second, he wipes his hand on his shirt and holds it out. I don't move. That makes him laugh.

"I'm Culler Evans," he says. "And you are Eddie Reeves."

I move back. "How do you know my name?"

"You look just like your father. I mean, when he was younger."

I lose myself for a minute, absorbing these extraordinary words, and then I search his face for the lie. Culler holds out his hand again.

"I'm Culler Evans," he repeats.

I stare at it for a second and then I shake it.

"Eddie Reeves."

"I'm . . ." he pauses. "I am unbelievably sorry about your dad."

"So you knew him."

Culler's hand comes to his Nikon. "I was his student."

"Oh . . ." I flush. "Sorry. I didn't—" I stop. "My dad didn't really take on students."

"I was an exception," Culler says. He doesn't sound like he's lying. "I'm not all that surprised you haven't heard of me. I know your dad preferred to keep his work to himself, separate from home . . . maybe not so much the opposite." I stare at him blankly. "I mean he loved to talk about you."

I don't even know what to say to that.

"It really wasn't my intent to startle you." Culler looks around and then points back to the building. "I know he spent a lot of time here, so I've been coming out, just trying to figure it all out, I guess. I mean, to understand why he'd . . ."

He trails off and my heart gets all excited. *Me too,* I want to tell him. *Every night. Every night, I come here.* But I don't. Not yet. Not *yet?* And then I realize in the time we've been talking, he is standing much closer to me than he was before.

I stare at his face. Twenty-one, maybe?

Twenty-two?

"You'll never figure it out," I tell him. "I haven't yet."

I should be scared. I'm too comfortable around Culler Evans, who says he knows my dad, who says he was his student. Maybe he's an obsessed fan. My dad used to get fan letters from a woman who said his work was her soul. She sent him naked pictures and she was sixty-five. For a while, my dad stuck them to the fridge. Mom loved that.

"We'll see," he says.

"Culler Evans," I say, trying to figure out if he is a lie.

"I sent a sympathy card. I met your mom once. Robyn."

Twenty-one. Maybe.

"How old are you?" I blurt out, and then I feel stupid. Culler stares at me, amused. I don't know why it even matters. "I mean, you look a little young to be my father's student . . ."

"Twenty." He holds up his camera and I cover my face instinctively. He laughs and says, "Camera shy? That's kind of funny."

"I don't even know you."

"Fair enough, Eddie Reeves."

He lowers the camera.

"How often do you come out here?" I ask him.

"How often do you?" he asks back.

I step back. This is insane. I need proof of Culler Evans's existence before this goes any further. It's not enough for him to stand in front of me and tell me things like this. I want to hear it from my dad, but I'll never hear it from my dad.

"I should go," I say abruptly.

"Think I'll stick around," he says. "The light's pretty great right now. But it was nice to meet you, Eddie Reeves." He studies me. "If I figure it out, I'll let you know."

I don't say anything. I bike toward the highway, my heart beating hard in my chest, and when I glance back, Culler is standing on the exact spot my father lay, watching me.

Mom and Beth are reminiscing over wine in the living room and Mom has been wasted for as long as she's been talking and laughing, so that's a couple of hours.

It's creepy, hearing her laugh. I'm so used to her silence.

I spend most of the evening avoiding them and looking for the sympathy cards that flooded the mail the first two weeks after Dad died. I have to search the whole house. I can't ask Mom where they are because I don't want asking her to be the difference between her being a happy drunk and a sad one, even though I'd rather she not be drunk at all.

I eventually find the cards strewn haphazardly in the very back of the junk drawer in the kitchen. I gather them up. They're still in the envelopes they came in because at some point, we have to send thank-you cards back, I think. *Thank you for your sympathy.* I set them in a neat pile on the table and find the envelope with Culler's name and address near the bottom of it. His card is white watercolor paper, folded in half. It's completely blank on the front.

I think I love it.

I think I love the idea that my dad's death could be so far

beyond any cheap sentiment you could put on the front of a sympathy card. I hope Culler meant it that way.

I open it up.

He is missed.
Culler Evans

I stare at the card for a long time, tracing over the letters with my finger. That's how I think it should be. Everything is complicated now but this is simple and true: he is missed. I want to go into the sympathy card business. I want all the cards to be like that. Forget sappy messages about overcoming; I want ones that say NOW YOU'LL BE A LESSER PERSON THAN YOU WERE or WE CANNOT POSSIBLY UNDERSTAND or I CAN UNDERSTAND BECAUSE SOMEONE I KNOW DIED TOO or maybe something about how grief can make your skin feel sore and bruised and electric because that's how my skin has felt ever since, except for my hands.

Mom cackles from the living room. I hear the clink of glass against the table and then she's slurring, "Oh no! No! Oh—God, get a paper towel, Beth!"

And then a knock on the front door.

I hastily put the cards back into the junk drawer.

"Someone's at the door," I call into the living room. Nobody says anything and the knocking persists. "I said someone's at the door. Maybe one of you should get it."

"We're busy." Beth. "So get it yourself please. And if it's anyone for your mother, tell them she can't talk right now."

"I can talk just fine, thank you very much," Mom insists, dissolving into giggles. "Do you want me to recite the alphabet?"

I close my eyes and count to ten.

Whoever is outside is still knocking.

Go away.

My cell chimes in my pocket. I answer it.

"Open the door already." Milo. "I'm not moving until you do."

I kind of thought so. I hang up and open the front door. He's there. At first, I cross my arms like I'm mad at him, but I don't think I am. I mean, I kind of am, but I don't know. I step onto the porch and close the door behind me.

"What?" he asks. "I'm not allowed inside now?"

"You don't want to go in there. Trust me."

"Oh. Okay."

"Yeah."

He sits on the steps and I sit beside him. Neither of us says anything for a minute and then he exhales slowly and rubs his hands together.

"Wish you'd stuck around today," he says. "Missy didn't stay that long."

"I was kind of caught off guard."

"So you're mad because I didn't tell you, right? That's what this is about?"

"How long did you know? Was it really May?" I ask. He doesn't say anything. I nudge him in the ribs. "Come on, how long did you know she was coming?"

"I knew at the end of May."

"My dad wasn't dead then."

"Yeah, but you got weird with me when I was with Missy—"

"I did not—"

"Yes," he interrupts, "you did. I never saw you. You just high-tailed it every single time she was around and we barely talked, we barely saw each other for—"

"Ten months," I finish.

"Exactly."

"Milo, she was your girlfriend," I say. "You *should* have been seeing her more than me. I mean, come on—you see it in movies all the time, where the girlfriend gets this hate-on for the best friend and then the guy has to choose—"

"*What?* Where did you get that fucking ridiculous idea? What makes you think Missy would've actually made me choose between the two of you?"

"Her name."

He snorts. "Nice."

"Seriously—*Missy?*"

"Melissa."

"She *tells* people to call her Missy."

"So? You have a boy's name."

"And you have a dog's name."

It's humid out. Too humid. I debate telling Milo about Culler, but I don't. Maybe I'll just wait, like he waited to tell me about *her.* That seems fair.

"So are you two back together while she's here or what?"

"We're just going to hang out for the summer," he says.

I think that means yes.

"You still could've told me sooner."

Silence. I hate this silence. I can't even stand it enough to appreciate the summer sounds all around us, and those sounds are one of my favorite things about this season. How gentle the breeze is, that soft rush. The way it moves the leaves on the trees. The crickets. The birds that haven't called it a day, not yet.

"Missy doesn't have a problem with you," Milo says. "You don't need to disappear."

I don't say anything. He nudges me until I look at him—three times—and when I look at him he seems so sincere and nice about it, it kind of makes me want to cry.

"Just don't," he says. "Okay?"

"My hands are still cold," I say stupidly. I don't know why. It's all I can think of to say and it's the one thing that never stops being true. I wish I knew how to make them warm again.

"Stop," Milo says. He shifts away from me a little and asks, "So where did you go? I mean, after you left."

"Nowhere."

"Nowhere," he repeats.

He's not buying it, but he leaves it at that. He rests his head on my shoulder. I lean into him. His hair is soft and smells like an unlikely combination of coconut and mint and I want to ask him what kind of shampoo he uses, but I know if I did, he'd just accuse me of sniffing his hair.

And then Beth totally ruins the moment by pushing through the door and gracelessly making her way down the steps to face us. Her cheeks are pink.

"Eddie," she says. "Can I talk to you for a minute? In private?"

"No," I say. Beth, half-smashed, wanting to talk to me privately. So many possibilities and none of them I am willing to subject myself to. "No way."

"Please," she says.

That should be my first real clue that something's not right because Beth never says *please* to me and means it, but I realize this too late.

"If you have something to say, say it."

"Fine. I need help getting your mother to bed. She's . . ." She pauses for a long moment, and then forces the next word out of her mouth slowly. "Incapacitated."

I stare. "How much wine did you *give* her?"

"Why does that matter?" she asks. "That's unimportant. It's moot now. I just need help getting her to bed. So will you help me or not?"

"Do it yourself."

"I *can't.*"

"Then why did you ask?"

Milo gets up. "I can help—"

"*No!*" I don't mean it to come out that way—that strangled, that urgent. They both look at me like I have three heads. My face burns. ". . . I don't want you to."

"Look, I'll do it," Milo says. "Eddie, it's not a big deal."

"Milo—"

He goes into the house before I can stop him. Beth fixes me with a haughty look.

"Maybe next time you'll listen to me when I ask to talk to you privately."

"What do you mean *next* time?"

I step inside the house. Beth follows. When I get to the living room, it's a nightmare. Two bottles of wine have been decimated. Milo hovers over my mom and she smiles at him, out of it, trying to get her arm around his shoulder.

It takes forever.

I watch them walk unsteadily across the floor, reaching the stairs at a snail's pace. My stomach shrivels into nothing. I don't want to see this.

"There's a step," Milo tells her in his most gentle voice. I bury my face in my hands. I don't want to hear it either. "That's great, Robyn. Okay, there's another step . . . great . . ."

"It didn't have to be this bad," Beth says after Milo and Mom finally disappear. I raise my head and glare at her. "You don't have to turn everything into a big scene. And look on the bright side: wine has lots of health benefits."

"Thanks so much, Beth. Really."

"Oh, *relax*. I haven't seen your mom that animated in forever."

"You got her *drunk*."

Beth shrugs. "Still. When was the last time you made her laugh?"

Ten minutes pass before Milo comes back down.

I can't even look at him.

"Thank you, *Milo*," Beth says pointedly. She pats him on the shoulder and fumbles past him. She smiles at the wine bottles. "That was fun. Like being back in college."

"You're not that young anymore," I tell her. "Every day you're farther from it."

She stops dead in her tracks and faces me very slowly.

I brace myself.

"Maybe you could clean this up, Eddie, if it's not too beyond you."

Her voice is cool, but it's all she says.

"It really wasn't a big deal," Milo assures me after she's gone. He walks over to the table and grabs one of the wine bottles. He holds it out to me.

"Still some left." He takes a swig and makes a face. "That is the most fucked-up wine I have ever tasted."

I grab the bottle from him. "It's not like you're an expert."

"I guess not."

He grabs the glasses and takes them into the kitchen. After a second, the water rushes—he's washing them—and I'm struck by how adult this all is and how tired that makes me. I should be wrecked. I should be upstairs, sleeping it off while Mom and Beth act like grown-ups down here. Instead, I just stand still, staring down the wine bottle until Milo comes back into the room and touches my shoulder. When I look at him I see that night—the one that changed everything—all over his face.

That night is the reason for this one.

"Did he seem unhappy to you?" I ask, clumsily turning the bottle over. I almost drop it. My stupid hands. "I mean . . . did he seem like he wanted to die?"

Milo takes the bottle from my hands. I can tell he doesn't like touching them. He thinks about it for a second and I imagine him searching through memories on memories for some sort of clue. Something he saw—something he saw that I didn't.

"He seemed like he always did," he finally says.

Which is a horrible answer the more I think about it.

It's a beautiful morning. Hangovers abound, so it's mine and mine alone.

I stay in bed for a long time, staring at the ceiling, my mind blank. Empty. That sounds depressing, but it's not. Sometimes you can think too much. I actually made myself sick the first three days after because I had thoughts bigger than the space that contained them and too many of them were happening at once. Sometimes the quiet is good. Most times not, but just for now, in this tiny moment where the sun is edging up the sky, it's okay.

And then I get out of bed.

I get out of bed and I get dressed.

I get out of bed and I get dressed and I go downstairs and I find a piece of blank paper and I fold it into a card. I stare at the empty space inside of it for a long time.

I grab a pen.

I'm sorry for your loss.
Eddie Reeves.

I hate when people say that to me, but this feels different because *I'm* the one writing it. It's more important. I want him to know it's not just me, that I know he must be in pain too.

That I understand.

I find Culler's address on the envelope he sent us. I tuck my card into a new envelope and address it to him, stamp it, and then leave the house on my bike and mail it.

When I get back, Beth is awake. She's making some complicated puke-green smoothie and she winces every time she pulses the blender. Every time she takes the lid off to see how it's coming along, she covers her mouth like she's going to barf. She does this so many times, I sit at the table and just watch, crossing my fingers that she'll vomit everywhere, just suffer some gross indignity while I'm there to witness it.

It doesn't happen.

When she finally acknowledges my presence she says, "There's a message on the answering machine."

"So?"

"So listen to it."

I walk over to the phone and press the play button. It doesn't occur to me that I should prepare myself for what I'm about to hear, even though Beth is the one who told me about it. Half of me is thinking maybe it's Culler. I don't know why. It's not.

"Uhm, hello Reeves family! This is Maggie Gibbard, at the studio. We have some things of Seth's here that we think you might want to come down and get . . . as soon as possible. It's just, we're in the process of renting the space again and we don't want anything lost in the shuffle. Also, we'll need the key back. Okay, please call us so we can figure this out. Thanks."

I stare at it.

"I don't think," Beth says carefully, pouring the green smoothie into a very tall glass, "your mother needs to hear that."

I'm going to pretend I don't know what's coming next.

"You could get down to Delaney, couldn't you? Milo could drive you or something? Get his things, return the key, drive back . . ."

Before I can tell Beth exactly what I think of that idea, Mom comes into the room. In Dad's housecoat. Her lips are a thin line on her pale face and her eyes are as sad as they always are. She's back to being a zombie. Beth hands her the green drink and gives me a look.

I delete the message from the answering machine.

Deacon Hunt is staring at me from his side of the room. His right hand is resting over his crotch and he's pressing down hard and *kneading* it with his fingers and acting like no one else can see him doing it, and I really wish I were making this up.

This is a party.

I don't like parties. Milo doesn't even really like parties. But when Missy said Deacon Hunt invited her to a party, it was only natural that she would drag Milo to it and, I guess, only natural that *he* would drag me. It's not natural that I would let him, but now that I share a living space with Beth, I can't be really picky about what gets me out of the house.

Anyway, Missy is in her element. She was born to party. Being here makes her happy.

This wasted Friday night makes her happy.

She's dancing with Milo. Grinding with him.

Deacon Hunt lives in a musty old retro farmhouse and I'm sitting on a grandma-style couch in the corner. It's weirdly soft, like velveteen, and it's striped orange and gold. It's next to a grandma-style floor lamp with plastic crystals lining the outside of the shade.

This is so lame.

After a while, Milo extricates himself from Missy, or she gets pulled away by yet another old friend who thinks it's *so awesome* she's *back* and by the way, she *looks fucking hot!*

"Do you want to leave?" Milo asks, sitting next to me.

"God no," I lie. "I'm having a great time."

And I can't make Missy leave before she's ready. We sit there watching her free-float, and I feel lonely. After a while, I lose sight of her movie-star frame and bleached-out hair and watch the minute hand on the grandfather clock in the corner move forward. I glance across the room and Deacon is still massaging his crotch.

"Deacon's hand has been on his dick and balls all night."

"He's wasted." Milo grins and I realize how long it's been since he's actually really smiled at me and that makes me feel worse, but good. But worse.

"Hey, Eddie. Hey, Milo."

Jenna Trudeau nods at us as she passes. I wave at her and then I realize something else: everyone here is talking about Missy's return, but no one here has said one thing about my father being dead. Even though it's nice not to talk about it, I think that makes these people assholes. I go to school with assholes. What kind of people wouldn't ask me about my dead father? Assholes.

After a while, Missy comes back, sparkling sweat.

"They're going swimming," she says. "Down at the lake. *Clothing optional.*"

"Wow," I say.

Milo holds up his hand. "I'll pass."

"Oh, come *on*."

She grabs our hands and tries to pull us up. I think I hate her. And then I feel bad for thinking that because Missy has a huge heart that's open to everything. She's not cynical.

That should be a beautiful thing.

"Please?" she whines. "I'm not going without you."

Milo glances at me. He waits for me to say it.

"Okay, sure." I sigh. "Whatever."

She squeals and grabs my hand. Grabs Milo's. Her palm is warm and alive and I let her lead me out of the house, into a pack of semi-sober almost-seniors who want to take it all off and get all wet, and there are so many reasons this is a bad idea, but I'm not here to save anyone's life. Milo is beside me. I can't tell if he's into this or not. I can't read him around Missy. She finally lets go of my hand, but stays holding on to his. I look around. There's about ten of us. The night air is sticky and smells swampy even though we're nowhere near a swamp.

Aaron Romero bounds up beside me.

"Getting naked, Reeves? Vinton?"

She laughs and I roll my eyes. "You wish."

"Of course I do. That's why I asked."

"I could get naked," Missy says. "Are *you*, Aaron?"

"I hope not," Milo says.

"Hey, fuck you, man," Aaron says. He trips over a rock and does a face-plant. Milo laughs and we move past Aaron, trudging farther and farther away from the house, down the road, eventually turning onto the trail that leads to Orbison Lake.

As soon as everyone sees the water, they turn into lemmings, rushing at it, laughing, whooping. Clothes go flying. I glimpse Missy's perfect ass and her perfect breasts before she disappears into the lake with the rest of them, having the time of her life.

"Weird," Milo says as soon as we're alone.

"What?" I ask.

"We'll have seen most of our senior class naked before school even starts."

I can't help but laugh. "Yeah."

Milo smiles at me again. I smile back and I get a weird feeling in my stomach. A smile and a laugh. These things feel wrong in their rightness. Distant splashing noises reach my ear. I look up. The sky is a black pool of ink, dotted with stars that look like they know where they're supposed to be. It makes me sort of dizzy.

I lose my footing and bring my heel down on the toe of Milo's shoe.

"Be careful." He steps back.

"What would you do if I died?" I ask.

"Where the fuck did that come from?"

I shrug. "I just want to know. Have you ever thought about it?"

I glance at him. He's staring at the ground, like he's spacing out. He stays like that for so long, I think I'll have to wave my hand in front of his face to bring him back, but I don't.

"No," he finally says. "I haven't thought about it."

"So think about it now."

"Stop it."

Moonlight is cast across the floating heads in the lake and there's nothing truly interesting about it. Missy swims next to Dale Mugford.

"Is that what you like?" I ask Milo.

"What?"

I point in Missy's direction. "That's what you like."

He doesn't say anything. I kick a little dirt at him and take my sandals off, curling my toes into the grit and grass that bleed down into a dirty bank that turns into the water. I should go in. I imagine myself swimming, all my clothes on and how heavy they'd feel. I imagine diving under, swimming down, down, down with my eyes open and not being able to see anything in front of me. Not even my hands. I imagine forcing myself farther down, until I feel weeds everywhere, brushing the sides of my arms, my feet, and then I'm surrounded. Tangled up in them so bad the lake would have me forever. I imagine drowning and what that would feel like, if I'd be scared. If I'd let it happen or if I'd fight it. I read in a book once you can't drown yourself. Your body will fight to survive, whether you want to or not.

But I don't think it's the same when you jump.

. . .

Aaron gets a bonfire going after the lake and by that time the crowd has thinned. It's me, Missy, Milo, Deacon, Aaron, Jenna, Mary Lennon, and Jeff Kingsley. Missy and Milo sit next to each other, so I sit on the other side of the fire and watch them touch shoulders through the flames because it's more dramatic that way.

I wonder if they've had sex yet.

Milo would die if he knew I thought that. Now and before. I thought about him and Missy having sex every single minute they were together the first time around, but not jealously. I *am* jealous of Missy in some ways, but not in that way. I just wonder about it. Imagine it. It might be weird, but it's not jealous. I think it's because I always thought Milo and I would be each other's first time. I secretly wanted it. I wanted us to be clumsy and bad and awkward with each other first, practice until we got crazy good, and then we'd stop and go find other people to impress in bed. Or whatever. But his first time ended up being with Missy and my legs never opened for anyone, which in Branford is probably not a bad thing.

"Yo, Eddie," Jeff says. I look up. He tosses a can of beer at me. I pull the tab and take a gulp. I don't like the taste of beer, but there are worse ways to be a follower, I guess.

"You know, this time next year we'll be getting ready to leave," Jenna says loudly enough to silence everyone around her. "One more year at BHS and then grad."

"Don't say that," Missy says.

"Do you like Pikesville High?" Milo asks her.

"It's nice. I've met some really great people. I have friends," she says. "But I don't know, being back here . . . I just miss you guys . . . a lot."

A chorus of sympathetic murmurs. Mary walks over and gives Missy a big hug and then Missy *cries*. She cries beautifully this side of the bonfire and Milo is looking at her with such . . . I don't know, such want, I think, and that's beautiful too. I hate that I'm so numb and empty and disconnected from most of these people but even I can see worth in stupid little moments like these. These people aren't even my family, but I can see their value and if I can see it in something this small, when I feel this bad, then—

Then why didn't he?

I take another sip of the beer. Try to distract myself from the knot in my throat and the fact that I feel like I'm going to cry.

"If I lived in Pikesville, I'd kill myself," Deacon mutters.

"Deacon," Jenna hisses.

I stare at the bonfire until I realize it's fallen uncomfortably quiet and everyone is staring at me. I have to replay the conversation to understand why and then I understand why.

"Oh. It's okay," I say to Deacon. I've just glimpsed what my life is going to become after the initial grief passes: people making jokes about offing themselves in front of me and apologizing for it after and then all the awkward silence that follows. "It's okay."

"Sorry about your dad," Deacon says. He doesn't look embarrassed or apologetic about what he said. All its potential offensiveness probably never would've occurred to him without Jenna's help. "That was supremely fucked up."

"Yeah," I agree. "It was."

"Is it true your mom's like, catatonic?"

"Deacon!" Jenna again.

"What?" Deacon asks. "It's not like we're not all thinking it." He turns back to me. "Jenna's plan of action once she found out you were coming was to shut the fuck up, basically."

"It's okay," I repeat.

It actually *is* okay. The casual way the questions roll off Deacon's tongue makes me want to answer them. It's like it's only us, him and me, talking about this. Everyone else slowly fades into the background until they're ghosts.

"She's kind of catatonic, I guess. She doesn't get dressed a lot."

"Did he leave a note?" Deacon asks. I nod. He gives an impressed whistle. "For a while there, my mom thought it had been a murder—"

"Okay," Milo says, not so much a ghost anymore. "That's enough."

"It's fine." I turn back to Deacon and sip at my beer. "My mom thought that too, for a minute. It just turned out we didn't . . ."

"Didn't what?" Deacon prompts.

I shrug. "You think you know someone and you don't." And then I take it a step further: "I mean . . . I don't know. You could all be jumpers. Wrist slitters. OD'ers. Stand in front of a train. I had no idea my dad was suicidal."

Missy shivers. "God, that's a terrible thought."

"Did you see it?" Deacon asks.

"Okay, *that's* the line," Aaron says. "You crossed it."

But everyone is staring at me, waiting for me to speak.

"I did," I say.

They all go so still. They all seem to stop breathing at once.

I clear my throat. "It was getting late and I knew he liked to go to Tarver's Warehouse sometimes. He'd spend *hours* out there, just taking photographs. Dinner was getting cold—he misses dinner all the time, so I don't know what made me go to get him this time . . . but I went and I get there and—" I finish off the beer and everyone is eating this up. "I saw him on top of the roof and he was doing something with his hands . . ." I shrug. "I don't know what he was doing with his hands. So I waved and I shouted and he looked up and he crossed his arms over his chest and he stepped off."

"How close were you?" Deacon asks, leaning forward.

They're all leaning forward.

"I heard it," I say.

Milo drops Missy off at home first. I like that. I'm in the back-seat, staring out the window, counting the tops of streetlights.

"Why did you lie to them?" Milo asks.

I shrug but I don't say anything.

After that, I become my mother.

Which means for four days I stop brushing my hair and live in my housecoat and shuffle around the house, mute and sad, and I don't answer my phone.

Milo sends me four text messages. One a day.

STATION'S BORING WITHOUT YOU. MISSY'S NOT HERE ALL THE TIME, WHATEVER YOU THINK.
COME OVER TODAY.
OR CALL ME.
ARE YOU OKAY?

The truth is, I'm fine. I'm kind of tired of everything, I guess, but I haven't given up—I'm only pretending to, so I can drive Beth insane.

It might be working. She says one hundred words for every three she manages to force out of my mom and every two she forces out of me and her eyes develop this panicked glint.

That's sort of cool.

Day four starts like: Beth bursts into my room and tries to wake me up. I keep my eyes closed, but I pick at the mattress, so she knows I'm awake—I'm just not responding to her.

"Eddie! Up!" She sits down on the edge of my bed and shakes my leg. "Up! Up! Up!"

She waits about five minutes for me to acknowledge her and when I don't, she gives up, gets off the bed, and leaves the room. That's nice. I stretch out and stare at the ceiling.

"Eddie!"

When I finally come downstairs, Mom is curled up on the couch with a book. When she sees me, she puts the book down and holds her arms out. I go to her and I let her hug me.

She kisses the side of my face and says, "I love you."

"I love you too, Mom."

Just that—it exhausts her. By the time I'm halfway out of the room, she's leaning back and her eyes are closed. Her chest rises and falls so purposefully it's like she's telling herself to breathe because she can't remember how to do it without thinking about it.

I shuffle into the kitchen, where Beth's washing dishes. There's a tall glass of orange juice at my seat, plus two vitamins. I'm vitamin-worthy now. Incredible. I sit down and stare at them and then I pick up one of the vitamins. Hold it up and study it. It's round and orange. Wouldn't it be amazing if it could fix everything? You put it on your tongue and let it dissolve. All your emotional trauma will end and that broken, cold dead soul will be alive again! And all your physical problems will be cured too. Cancer, illness. Vitamins made out of Nanobots or something, I don't know.

"You need a boost," Beth says of the vitamins. She turns the water off and faces me. "I want you out of the house today."

"What?"

"Get dressed, get out of the house," she says. "I let you laze about for three days, but don't think you'll be spending the summer like that because you won't be."

"What?"

"You're not spending the rest of summer vacation sleeping in late, hanging around inside, breathing recycled air and—" Her eyes travel over me and I can't believe she's mistaken my fucking *grief* for *laziness*. "Not brushing your hair. I don't know if you spend every summer like this, but it doesn't matter. I need you out of the way while I help your mom. Besides, this isn't the kind of time you should be wasting. Go! Live!"

I imagine so many horrible things happening to her.

There's a dirty, rusty old station wagon parked in the muck at Tarver's.

I press my face against the driver's side window and look in. There's a Coke in the drink holder and crumpled fast food wrappers scattered on the passenger seat. On the floor, a nickel catches the sunlight and glints at me. In the backseat, there's a discarded jacket and an iPod and a couple of paperbacks with the front covers ripped off.

"Hi, Eddie."

I step back. Culler is rounding the building, lowering his camera. I know instantly he's taken my photo and he knows I know it. He points behind him. "I couldn't tell it was you from way back there. I took the shot just in case you were stealing my car."

"Not stealing it." I shove my hands in my pocket. "I thought it was your car." I pause. "I mean, I knew it was your car."

He stops a few feet from me.

"Thank you for the card," he says.

"It was nothing."

"No, it was really nice. And I appreciate it." He looks away. "I do miss him."

"I just thought . . ." I shrug. "I mean, sometimes I forget I'm not the only one."

"Well, in a way you are. You're his only daughter."

"I guess. Thank you for your card . . ."

"Of course."

"So, did you figure it out?" I ask.

"Nope. You?"

"No . . ."

He squints at me. "He leave a note?"

"Would you believe that's the second time I've been asked that in less than a week?"

"I'd believe that."

I swallow. "He did."

"I won't ask you what it said," he says, which is good, because I don't want to tell him it didn't say anything. It didn't say why. He leans against the car and taps his fingers against his Nikon and stares up at the sky. "What do you come out here for, besides that?"

"What do you mean?"

He pats the side of the car. I lean beside him.

"I take photos," he says. "Just knowing it inspired him; that he came here to be inspired . . . I'm hoping to feed off that. You don't take photographs, do you?"

I shake my head. "Does that surprise you?"

"No," Culler says, smiling. "Did you ever really get how famous he was at a certain point in his life? Within certain circles? I've always wondered what it must be like to have a kind of celebrity parent. Can their kids ever understand that scope? Their impact?"

"Probably not."

"Your father changed my life."

"Wow," I say, but I'm not being sarcastic. I mean it.

Culler looks to the building. It's silent and I don't want it to be silent. I want to hear him talk more. I want to hear him talk more about my dad.

"It was all over when I was born," I say.

Culler nods. "He told me he liked Branford because no one understood."

That's something I've heard my dad say before. He chose Branford because it's not that the people here are or were unaware of his past, it's that it's almost too big for so small a place. Beyond comprehension. Or maybe it really is that no one cares.

He liked it here, anyway.

"If I was him, I'd stay where people understood," Culler says. "I'd never walk away."

I rub my arm. ". . . Do you think he hated the work?"

"God, no," Culler says. "He hated the community, sharing his work. If he hated the art, he would've stopped. But he kept going. He was constantly looking for inspiration."

Our eyes meet. We're both thinking the same thing.

"Maybe he loved the work," I say, "but couldn't find inspiration anymore."

"*That* would be a good reason to off yourself," Culler says.

I am not a creative person. I used to be embarrassed to say so. It's just not the way I think. I can't draw, I don't sing, I'm not a photographer or a writer or anything. Some people just aren't. I'm one of them. I can appreciate art, though. I've been moved by it. I try to imagine what it must be like to have art inside of you and then to not have it anymore. To lose it, to not be able to find it, to search for it . . .

Maybe that *is* a good reason to kill yourself.

And now I want this possibility out of my head because it makes my chest ache. It makes me want to cry. It makes me want to scream.

But I'm quiet beside Culler. I'm not even breathing.

"But I don't think that was his reason," Culler says after a minute, but there's a tinge to his voice, like he doesn't totally believe it.

"What was it about this place?" I ask. "That kept him coming back to photograph it?"

"No idea."

We stare at the building.

There is nothing about this place.

"Eddie," he says after a minute. "Can I show you something?"

I stare at him and he stares at me. Last time, I would have said no, but now we've exchanged sympathy cards so I guess that changes everything.

"Okay," I say.

He walks across the lot wordlessly, and I guess I'm supposed to follow after him, so I do. The closer we get to the warehouse, the more uneasy I feel. My stomach is cold. When Culler gets to the entrance, the two massive, rusting doors at the front, I know he wants to go in.

I feel dizzy.

"I—"

I stop.

Culler turns. We stand like that, about five feet between us. He stares at me for a long minute. The breeze picks up and brushes my hair against my face and he raises his camera to his eye and snaps a photograph, startling me.

"Sorry," he says. "You were a perfect photograph."

"It's okay," I mumble, even though I'm not sure it is, but I remember my father's random bursts of inspiration, the ones that had him kissing us frantically on the cheeks and running out of the house. Except I can't quite believe I'd inspire a photograph. "I can't go on the roof."

"Oh," he says.

"I just . . . can't."

"I would've never asked you to."

"Okay."

"It is inside, though. What I want to show you," he says. He holds out his hand. "Let me show you, Eddie. It wouldn't be right if I didn't."

I stare at his hand for what feels a long time and then I put my palm against his, but my fingers stop working again. I can't actually hold his hand. Culler doesn't even blink or ask me why—he just closes his fingers around mine, simple as that, and in that moment it's electric. I am touching someone who really understands. I can do this. I can go in.

I will let him show me whatever he wants to show me.

He lets go of my hand and pulls the doors open. The entrance into Tarver's is like a black hole, even though it's day, even though light is pouring in through the windows. Death has been here and where death has been no light shall ever be.

Or something.

Culler takes my hand again and walks me inside.

I don't know anything about the history of Tarver's Warehouse. What people did here. How they worked. Who they worked for. Why. I never thought to ask my father and my father never thought to tell me. The place is empty and strange and echoey and dusty. Really dusty. I sneeze and instantly feel like I've broken the sacred-ness of this moment.

Culler leads me away from the center of the room and down the side of the wall. The ground is concrete and dirty and full of debris. I step over pieces of wood. I have no idea where they came from. Eventually, we get halfway through the building.

"How do you get onto the roof?" I ask, fighting the nausea the question inspires.

"You just keep going up," Culler replies. He points to a door on the opposite wall. "There are stairs behind there. What I want to show you is over there. I just want to take you to the door, though. Not through it."

I nod, but I don't feel nearly as steady about this as I look.

It's different in the day. I've been inside at night, when everything looks like nothing, no color. In the light, I see the door is faded red and I know every time I see red from now on, I'll think of my father's death. Culler takes my hand and then he presses it against the space just above the doorknob. There's a difference in texture. I notice it immediately.

We stand there.

He takes my photograph and before I can tell him to stop, he says, "Lower your hand," and I do, and then he says, "Do you see it?"

Etched into the rotting wood—maybe by a key, something—*S.R.*

I feel like someone has turned my head off, my heart.

I face Culler, my mouth open, but I'm not sure what I should say.

"Did you put that there?" he asks.

"What? No—"

"I didn't either."

I turn back to the scratch marks. The name. I can't believe this. I press my hand over the letters again, rub my palm over them and try to feel them—more.

I suck in a breath and pull my hand away.

"What?" Culler asks.

I shake my head and stare at my palm. My hand is shaking and a little splinter has planted itself directly into that soft space of skin just under the base of my thumb. It stings. Culler steps forward and sees it. He uses his fingernails to try to dig it out.

Too many things are going on in my head.

"He put it there," I say.

"Yeah," Culler says. "I think so."

"When?"

"I don't know."

"The night he died?" I ask him this like he would know the answer.

"Maybe." He finally gets the splinter out. He looks at me and his eyes are intent. "Maybe not."

"S.R.—that's like—"

"*Secrets on City Walls,*" Culler says. "He'd put those photographs up everywhere and they'd have his initials on them. First thing I thought of too."

I stare at the scratches. "But . . . why would he do that?"

"I don't know. I just wanted to show you."

I feel lightheaded.

"Are you okay?" Culler asks. I must look like I'm spacing.

"Uhm . . . I have to go to his studio. I have to clear it all out," I say. "Everything."

"309 Hutt Street. Delaney," he says.

"How did you know?"

He smiles faintly. "Where do you think I learned?" And then I flush and he frowns. "They want you to clear it out already?"

"They're renting the space . . . they don't want anything to get lost in the shuffle . . ."

"Maggie Gibbard, right?" he asks. "She's full of it. She just wants it gone. Twit."

"Maybe." But I don't really have a problem with Maggie. ". . . And my mom can barely get out of bed, so it's just me. I have to get his stuff. I don't even have a way down there."

"I could take you," he says.

Which is exactly what I wanted him to say.

'm slowly edging down the roof when Milo's car pulls up in front of the house.

He sees me.

There's not a whole lot I can do about it. He stares up at me from the driver's side, his mouth open, like he can't believe what he's stumbled upon. I guess it must look strange. I don't know why. We see this stuff in movies and television shows all the time.

Anyway, he just sits there, in his car, watching, and I have to jump. I feel self-conscious, wrong, doing it in front of him. I land hard but easy. I straighten and brush my legs off.

Milo gets out of the car.

"Do I even want to know?"

"Taking the front door isn't nearly as exciting," I say.

"Beth give you a curfew?"

"What are you doing here this late?" I ask him.

"What are you doing climbing out of a window and scaling down a roof this late?" Before I can say anything he says, "Or maybe a better question: why are you ignoring me, and does climbing out of a window and scaling down a roof have anything to do with it? Because I'm *really* curious now."

"I'm not ignoring you."

"Yes, you are. Since Deacon's," he says. "I texted you four times and you didn't get back to me. If this is about Missy—"

"You think a lot of yourself, don't you? Like, whatever anyone does, it's got to be about you and Missy, blah, blah, blah," I say, and it throws him off a little. His face turns red. "Maybe I just didn't feel like talking to you."

"What did *I* do?"

"You didn't do anything. But you're the only person I talk to, right? So when I don't feel like talking . . . you're the one I'm not talking to. It just works out that way."

"Most of the time you can't shut up," Milo replies, but he's referring to a time before my dad died. We stare at each other for a good minute and I'm stuck. I don't know what to do about this. I had a plan and now I have Milo and he's going to ask: "Where were you going?"

I shrug. "I just wanted out."

"Then my timing is impeccable, because I just got out of the Star with Missy. They had a double feature tonight. *The Blob* followed by *Night of the Living Dead*. Awesome." I bite the inside of my cheek because Milo and I probably would have gone to see those movies together if Missy were back in Pikesville, where she belongs. "I dropped her off at her grandparents' and decided I was hungry and *then* I decided I'd ask you if you wanted to go to Chester's with me."

"Are you paying?"

Milo laughs. "Sure."

"Is Missy okay with that? I mean, if you pay for me, does that make it a date?"

"Fuck off," he says, but he's smiling. I round the car and get into the passenger's side. Milo gets into the front and a moment later, my house is behind us.

"So how are things with Missy?" I try to keep my voice neutral.

"She's still very nice," he says.

"Her boobs got really big, didn't they?"

"Eddie—"

"What? They did."

He pauses. "Yeah."

"I wish mine were that big."

"Yours are—" He stops before he can finish, and I burst out laughing and I say, *I knew it, I knew it, you totally check me out all the time,* and then he starts laughing, pointing one hand at me and driving with the other. "You totally set me up! I wasn't thinking when I said that—"

"But mine are what? Please finish the sentence—"

"Just for that, *you're* paying for the food."

"Can't," I say. "I didn't bring my wallet."

"Very convenient."

I settle back into the seat, smiling. I roll down the window and let the warm breeze fill the car, even though Milo has the air conditioner cranked. This is good. This feels good.

This is like before.

And then my heart does a complete 180 on the moment and it's like it's *too* good.

It's too good.

How can things be so good they're bad? That's so stupid. And yet I feel this sadness encroaching, getting close. This isn't good. This is the *illusion* of good. Outside of this sweet moment with Milo is Missy stealing my best friend away, is my father six feet under the ground, is my mother, who can't stop wearing his housecoat, is Beth, who tonight decided she wants to take me to the mall so I can get my hair cut because I need a change because there hasn't been *enough* change in my life right now.

And it's so depressing.

I watch Branford drift past the window and I cry, which is embarrassing, but it's not like I make a production out of it. Milo doesn't even notice. I just sit beside him and hope my eyes don't get all red and gross looking and then, when we pull up to Chester's, I wipe at my face and get out of the car before he can take a good look at me.

Chester's is a small-town dive, but no one would ever call it that to eighty-year-old Chester McClelland's face. It's a restaurant. It's open twenty-four hours. It tastes like home, and home is greasy burgers and off-brand ketchup and fries that are so dry they turn to dust in your mouth.

The place is mostly empty. I recognize a few plaid shirts. Milo and I head for the booth at the very back. Our booth. I squeeze myself into the corner, against the wall. I like to make myself small in these booths, which haven't changed in the seventeen years I've been alive. I loved their enormity, the way they dwarfed me when I was a kid, sitting next to my dad. . . .

Once I asked Milo if he could, would he go back to being, like, five or seven, and he looked at me like I was nuts and I tried to explain: *it was simpler, right? It was. Don't you ever want to go back to that?* He didn't get it and that was when I realized a fundamental difference between us. I don't think Milo really worries about anything, doesn't wish for simpler times, because everything with him *is* simple. Sometimes that makes being around him feel good. Other times, it makes me so jealous of him, I could puke.

I twist around in the seat, try to bring my knees up, and realize something terrible: I can't make myself small in this booth anymore.

I don't feel small in this booth anymore.

The late-shift waitress takes our order. Gina. I keep my face to the window and let Milo request the usual: French fries smothered in fake cheese. A huge basket to split between us. We never wait for the cheese to cool. It burns our tongues. We chase each fry with a swig of Coke.

"When was the last time we came here?" I ask after Gina sets the fries in front of us. I can't remember when the last time we came here was.

Milo hesitates. "Before."

"Don't," I say.

"Don't what?" He reaches for a fry.

"Don't divide me into before and after."

"Well, it was—"

"May? It was May."

"It wasn't June," he mutters.

When my dad killed himself.

"Then it must have been May."

"So almost two months."

"Two months," he agrees.

I take a fry. The cheese scalds the back of my throat. It tastes different. I take a swig of Coke, swish it around in my mouth, and look around the place. It really is empty, dingy. Dirty.

I know it's a dive, but I can't remember it ever being *this* . . .

This.

"Beth wants to take me to the mall and get my hair cut," I say suddenly, because I don't want to think about how different Chester's has become and when it got that way, and why I didn't notice. "She said I need a fresh face. I thought she was going to suggest a chemical peel . . ."

Milo laughs and scarfs down more fries. "What's the logic there? That there's too much *sadness* tied to the way you look now?"

"Something like that."

Actually, I think the real reason Beth is tired of it is because she knows I make faces at her from behind a curtain of hair. But then, I also heard her telling Mom that since we can't afford to move to a new house where no one's decided they wanted to kill themselves, we should consider changing the furniture around. So who knows. Who cares.

"How do you think I should get it done?" I pull my hair back. It's long and brown and could do for a cut, but I'll die before that happens on an outing with Beth. "Bleach it? Turn it blond? Curl it just a little? I can be Marilyn too."

He stares. "Are you jealous of Missy or what?"

"I'm not fucking jealous of Missy Vinton." I laugh a little. If you're jealous of someone, you want what they have. I don't want what she has.

But I think I hate her and I don't even really know why.

Maybe I hate her because there's nothing about her to really hate.

"Then why do you say shit like that to me?" he asks.

"I'm just teasing you," I say. He keeps staring at me. Blankly. I can handle this place being different, but I don't think I can handle Milo being different in this place. "Jesus. Lighten up."

He raises his hands. "Maybe stop saying shit like that to me."

"Touchy. Gonna do an old-fashioned long-distance thing? Send letters to Pikesville?"

"Fuck off," he says.

"If I lived in Pikesville," I tell him, "I'd kill myself."

"Eddie." Milo leans forward. "Where were you going tonight that you had to sneak out?"

"Why not ask me where I'm going tomorrow instead?"

"Where are you going tomorrow?"

"I have to go to Delaney," I say. I pick up some fries, but my appetite has abandoned me. I force them into my mouth anyway. The cheese is already cooling, congealing. I swallow. "I have to pick up all of my dad's stuff."

"How are you getting down there?"

I pause. I still haven't told Milo about Culler, but there isn't a whole lot to tell and part of me likes keeping him a secret. I don't know. But that part of me is not the reason I lie to him.

I say, "Beth will be driving me down."

I wait for him to offer to take me because if he doesn't that means two hours to Delaney in a car with Beth and however long it will take to organize and pack up all of my father's things. Two hours back. He should want to save me from that. A fate worse than death.

"Oh," he says.

He should be offering to take me.

"Two hours to Delaney in a car with Beth," I say.

"That sucks."

"She'll have to go through his things with me."

He should be offering to take me.

Offer to take me, Milo.

"And then two hours back . . ."

But he doesn't.

But he knows I want him to, which makes it worse.

"Me and Missy," he says awkwardly. "Tomorrow, we're going—"

"Your tomorrow already sounds way more interesting than mine," I interrupt. "So maybe stop talking about it."

There are certain benefits to being best friends as long as we have—like how Milo understands my tone means I am so done with being here and talking to him and that right in this second, I don't care if I ever talk to him again, which is not entirely true but—

I'm angry.

"It's getting late," he says, because he knows.

"Thanks for the fries."

"It was nothing."

We leave. He drives back the way we came.

"Do you want to know where I was going?" I ask. "Where I was sneaking off to?"

"Of course I do." He glances at me and forces a smile. "I hate the idea of you sneaking off anywhere without me."

"I'll show you," I say.

"Okay."

"Okay, just, uhm . . . turn left before my street and keep going. Then take Ramos Street out to the highway, drive until you reach the second intersection, and then go . . ." I watch his grip tighten on the steering wheel and I should stop, but I can't stop. "Two miles. Turn right on a dirt road, go down it for a while until you see a ware—"

"Stop it," he says. "That's not—" He shakes his head. He doesn't turn left before my street. He drives down it and pulls up to my house. "You were going to Tarver's."

"Take me there."

"No."

"Why? Have you even been back there since—"

"*No,*" he snaps. He looks at me and his expression takes me aback. He's angry. "But you have, I take it. So how often do you go back there? You walk?"

"I bike."

"How often?"

I shrug.

"In the middle of the night?"

"Sometimes in the day." I turn to him. I want him to understand, but I already know I've lost this, that I should have never opened my mouth. But something important happened and I need to share it with him. "But, look, Milo, you won't believe this—but inside, I found this spot where my dad carved his initials into a door—he must've etched it right in there and—"

"*So?*" Milo asks.

"So—he was *there!*"

"For Christ's sake, Eddie, we know he was there—he jumped off the fucking roof!" I flinch and he sees it. His face softens and he reaches for me, but I jerk away from him. "Sorry—I'm sorry—I just—I don't know why you'd want to do something so *morbid*—"

"It's *not* morbid!"

"Yes, it *is*." He rubs his face. "And even if it wasn't, why the fuck would you *do* something like that to yourself—"

"Oh, fuck off, Milo." I unbuckle my seat belt. "Why does anyone do anything? Why do they jump off the top of buildings? I'm just trying to understand—"

"How will that help you understand?"

I open the door and move to get out when Milo grabs my arm and pulls me back. I sigh and sit back, staring determinedly at the roof. There's a little burn mark directly overhead, like someone put out a cigarette there a long time ago. I was with Milo the day he bought this car. Secondhand. He'd been saving for it forever, and when he got the keys, he told me he'd take me anywhere. Just say the word.

I know some friendships can't withstand horrible things happening, no matter how strong you think they are. People will never lose the ability to surprise you. I read it on some Web site about how other people will react to your grief and these four words stuck with me:

Your constants may falter.

"Please tell me about that night," I blurt out, just in case he falters even more and I never have the chance to ask him this again and again and again until he answers.

"No," he says.

"Why?"

"Why do you need me to tell you?"

I can't explain to Milo why I want to hear it from him. Some pieces are missing, and I know he has them. He knows I can fill in the blanks without him, but I also just want to hear him say it, like how I needed to be in the room with my mom when she called each one of our family members and friends to tell them what happened. That was when she could still talk easy, before the weight of it hit her, and I sat with her, holding her hand, pretending to be supportive when really I was waiting for her to say that one thing that would help me understand, even something as weak and incomplete as, *well, I knew Seth had been sad for a while . . .*

But that never happened.

With Milo, his refusal to talk about it makes me want to hear it from him more. Every time he doesn't, it's like I feel him going away from me, and that is more scary than I have words for. Losing someone who's not even dead.

And I want to say it, but I get out of the car and say, "I'll see you later," instead.

"Eddie." I turn. He leans across the seat and the look on his face—my heart stops. He looks like he'll say it—he'll tell me. But then his face changes. "It's not safe at Tarver's. The place is falling apart."

"Don't worry," I tell him. "I haven't gone up on the roof. Yet."

I slam the door shut and he just gives me this *look* and drives away.

That was probably the wrong thing to say.

go to Tarver's like I planned because nothing will stop me once I get it in my head.

I don't care what Milo says.

I stand in front of the door my father carved his name into, dizzy and sick, and I try so hard to get past it, but I can't move. I feel the weight of the building on me and imagine myself on the roof.

I imagine he's waiting for me.

told Culler to pick me up at Fuller's.

I don't know what's wrong with me that I'd ask him to do that.

But before that moment where Milo watches me get into a grimy-looking station wagon with Culler Evans, I have to get ready *for* that moment and I tear apart my closet looking for something nice to wear before I realize I'm trying to turn collecting the last vestiges of my dead father's post-career-career into a fake date just to provoke Milo into . . . I don't know.

I change into jeans and a tank top.

Mom and Beth are in the backyard. Beth wants to make sure she and Mom get fifteen minutes of sun a day, because that's healthy. She wanted to go to the park and have a picnic, but she still hasn't managed to get Mom out of her housecoat, so they're out in the backyard, in lawn chairs instead. A compromise.

I don't think Mom knows what I'm doing today, which is how it has to be, but I can't leave without telling them I'm going somewhere.

When I reach the backyard, Mom and Beth are sun-soaking statues. They're wearing sunglasses and hats, which I think must defeat the purpose, but they're still and their faces are pointed up. It's very quiet. Mom almost looks normal, if I ignore the fact that the corners of her mouth are pulled down. I clear my throat. They both turn their faces to me.

I'm the sun.

"I'm going out for a while," I say. "With Milo. I might not be back until later tonight."

"Where—" Beth starts, but I give her a pointed look and she gets it. "Oh."

"That's too bad," Mom says, and my stomach twists. Her voice is always a shock to me. Sometimes I think I forget it, even though I know I must hear it more than I think I do. "I was going to ask you to join us out here . . ."

Sometimes I have dreams about my mom holding me. It's really dumb and I wake up so angry because I don't dream about my dad and I want to.

"Maybe some other time," I say, and Beth gives Mom a knowing look like, *teenagers.* I hate her so much sometimes—I'm so full of it—that I'm amazed my brain can send any other kinds of messages to my body, like *move,* like *walk away.* Like *breathe.*

"Have a good time with Milo," Mom says.

I nod and then I walk around the side of the house and make my way to Fuller's and by the time I get there, I feel a little sick about it. I don't think I want to do this to Milo.

I mean, I *do.*

But I don't.

So I sit on the curb a little ways away. Far enough away not to get hit by people who need to fill their tanks and close enough that I won't have to run a mile to reach Culler's car when he finally pulls up. I check my watch. I'm a little early. I rest my chin in my hands.

He should be here soon.

"Eddie?"

I look up at my name. Missy stands over me. I didn't even hear her come up. She seems big from this angle. Really curvy. It's crazy.

It's not fair she's this curvy and I'm totally flat. I glance down the road. I hope Culler doesn't come while she's still out here.

"Hi, Missy," I say.

"What are you sitting out here for? Are you going to see Milo?"

"Nope."

She bends down so we're eye level.

"Why? That's where I'm headed. Come with me."

"No."

"Why not?"

"I've got plans."

"With who?"

"Doesn't matter. They're my plans, not yours." That was unnecessarily bitchy, despite the part of me that enjoyed it. I turn to her and try to look as earnest as possible. "I'm in a fight with Milo, so it's probably best if I keep my distance right now. Go without me."

"What did you fight about?" She sounds genuinely surprised.

"It's between me and Milo." I force a smile at her. "Don't worry about it. It's not a big deal. Just go, Missy."

"Okay," she says uncertainly. She straightens and makes her way to Fuller's. Her heels are clacking against the pavement as she goes. That's ridiculous. I stare at the tennis shoes on my feet. Who wears heels when they don't have to? And then the clacking stops and she turns back to me. "It's too bad, though. I like it when you hang around with us."

When *I* hang around with *them*.

I wave my hand and say *really* loudly, "*Bye,* Missy!"

She goes. Finally. About ten more minutes pass. When I spot the station wagon making its way up the street, I hear my name again.

"Hey, Eddie!" I get to my feet. Milo is standing outside Fuller's. Half-outside, half-inside. He's holding the door open. "Eddie! Hey!"

"What do you want?" I call to him. The station wagon pulls up beside me. I wipe my suddenly sweaty palms on my jeans.

"We're in a fight?"

"Yeah."

"Good to know," he calls. I round the station wagon and open the door. Milo frowns. "Who's that?"

I wave at him and I get in the car. My heart is beating fast. I turn to Culler and I smile at him, but that feels instantly weird. This is not a happy trip. But Culler smiles back at me. He has nice teeth. Today he is wearing a black T-shirt. Black jeans. Ray-Bans.

I wish I could see his eyes.

"Fuck me," I say suddenly, and his smile vanishes and my face turns red. "I mean—I forgot the studio key. I have to give it back. Maggie asked."

"It's okay," Culler says, pulling away from the curb. "I have a key." He glances at me. "Your dad made me a copy. We'll leave it for them and you can keep his. You shouldn't have to give something like that up."

I don't know what to say. It's such a nice thing for him to offer. But horrible. It never occurred to me to want to keep my father's key, but now it seems like the most obvious thing in the world. It meant something to him; it should mean something to me.

"Thank you for driving me down," I say.

"Thank you for letting me drive you," he says. "Thought the last time I'd see that studio was the week before he died. I wouldn't have felt right going in there with him gone."

With him gone. These are sad words.

"You worked in the studio?" I ask.

"I watched him work in the studio. I would bring my stuff down to show him. My darkroom is digital. It's all set up at my place—"

"Where do you live in Haverfield?" I interrupt. "Do you live alone?"

Culler laughs.

"You don't know anything about me, do you?"

I blush. "Sorry—"

"It's okay."

But it's not okay. I can't reconcile this gap in knowledge. That there is someone out there who maybe misses my dad as much as

I do, and I never heard about him. Or maybe I did and I just didn't pay attention. Dad, mentioning some student—the first student he'd ever taken on—at some point, and Culler's name going over me, because it wasn't important because it didn't affect all the stupid little things I was doing every day.

And now, here he is. Culler Evans. I don't know anything about Culler Evans.

And Culler Evans makes me realize how little I know about my father.

"I should've asked him." I can't breathe around the idea that there are all these things I don't know and I never thought to ask, will never get to ask. Who do I get those missing pieces from and will they ever be as good, or as whole, if they come from someone who isn't him? "How he felt about his photography and everything— why didn't I . . ."

"Don't sweat it," Culler says. "That's how kids are with their parents. It's natural. My dad's a surgeon and that's about all I can tell you. The man's *saved* people's *lives*. I think he's in a book about something he did. . . ." Culler laughs. "I just proved my point, didn't I? It's like what I said to you—you'll never understand the scope of your dad's career because he's your dad."

"That doesn't make me feel better."

Culler pauses. "Don't let it get you down. I know just about everything you don't and I worked with him. I'm just as . . . lost about this whole thing as you are."

I feel so bad for that, a total jerk, but I don't know what to say to make it better. At first I want to tell him that maybe between the two of us, we'll come up with something, but that almost seems too forward and I'm not sure I believe it.

Instead, I ask, "How did you end up becoming his student?"

"I e-mailed him, believe it or not."

"How did you get his e-mail address?"

He smiles. "I'm not telling you or you'll think I'm a stalker."

"How about a determined fan?"

"I'll take that. I live in this apartment in Haverfield," Culler says. Haverfield is halfway between Branford and Delaney. "And your dad was my idol. His work was incredible. The way he arrived on the scene—he just wanted to share his art. That was it. And he did. And then the way he left, when he started feeling compromised, he just cut through the bullshit and went."

"Yeah," I say.

"And it drove me crazy that he was close, so I got his e-mail and I e-mailed him and I told him he was the reason I wanted to be a photographer. I offered to assist him for free if I could learn from him. I have an online portfolio, so he checked it out. He said he liked my artist's statement and agreed to take me on as a student."

"What's your artist's statement?" I ask. "Where do you go to school?"

Culler laughs. I like the sound of it.

I like that he can laugh despite where we're going and what we'll do when we get there.

"I don't go to school for this. I don't care about school. I care about *art*, about sharing it. Art is to be shared . . . that's my objective. Sounds familiar, I know."

"Vaguely," I say.

"That's why all my work goes online. He said I reminded him of him, except more uncompromising. He said it was good I figured out how to put myself out there on my own terms. He'd never be able to do that, because of his legacy."

My stomach twists. "You think that's why—"

"No," Culler interrupts. He takes off his glasses and sets them on the dash. He glances at me and I like his eyes. I like his eyes when they're looking at me. "Eddie, if I can promise you anything, I promise you, he loved his work."

"Okay," I say.

"Anyway, he called me a raw talent—an intuitive photographer, which is a nice way of saying I'm completely ignorant about the technical aspects of photography, but a good photo is a good photo, right? He'd let me observe him at work and gave me advice on how to get the photos I wanted to shoot out of my head. It was kind of informal, but it was absolutely incredible . . . he made me believe I could do this for real and until I met him I wasn't always sure." He pauses and clears his throat. "But now I'm sure. That's what I mean when I say your dad changed my life."

"I'm glad you met," I say honestly.

"Me too. I love the way he told stories. Plastered them all over city walls just to get them out there," he says. "And that's what I want to do, at any cost. I want to share my stories. He respected that. It's about putting what's inside of you out there." Maybe it's a trick of the light, but he almost looks like he could cry and that makes my throat tight. "I haven't, though, since he died."

"How come?" I ask.

"Nothing seems important enough anymore." He reaches for his glasses and puts them back on. "Now I just want to know why. I need to know why."

The way to Delaney is mostly fields and farms, horses, cows, guinea hens, until it is suddenly, miraculously, a city that is not really much more special than a town like Branford, except it has a mall, and every fast-food chain you could ever want to eat at. And a studio, where four artists gather—no, three . . .

"Me too," I tell him. "More than anything."

There's nothing else until I know why.

The studio is a brick building with huge windows just on the outskirts of Delaney. It's two stories. The first story is a kind of common area, with separate work spaces. The second story is where the photography happens. There's a darkroom and a long stretch of space for shoots and equipment. Background paper, lights, soft boxes, umbrellas, and so much other stuff I can't even remember the names of—I've only been here a handful of times in my life and like I said, I'm no artist. I almost tell Culler about the time I accidentally walked in on one of Maggie's shoots, but I'm glad I think better of it because it was something naked and bondage-y.

I was fifteen.

When Culler and I let ourselves in, Maggie is in the kitchen area, flipping through a magazine. The place is pretty messy, considering so few people work in it. But it's artfully messy. Pretentiously messy. Artists work here.

"Have you got the key?" Maggie asks. That's how she greets us. Maggie is a lithe blond thing. She's twenty-seven. Her work is about sex and gender and violence. I used to love her photos, loved sneaking looks at them and marveling over all of the ways people can fuck and pose and not look like they're posing.

"Always so good to see you, Maggie," Culler says, digging into his pocket. He tosses the key at her. It hits the table, slides off, and lands on the floor at her feet.

"I didn't know you two were friends," Maggie says. "Hi, Eddie."

"Where is everyone?" I ask.

"Rick's not here, surprise, surprise," she says. Rick Vance is closest to my dad's age, maybe a little younger. He had his day, I guess, but now he hardly ever works. He pays for the space just in case. Dad used to say he was waiting for Rick to realize his heart wasn't in it, but he was fine with Rick paying rent until he did. "And Terra's shooting upstairs, so you can't go up there right now, but it doesn't matter—your dad's stuff is down here anyway."

She says this so casually, like it's nothing. Like I'll just get what my father left behind and take it to the house, where he's alive and waiting for me.

Not like he's dead and this is what's left of him.

"Jesus, Maggie," Culler says, and I am so glad he's here with me for this. "Your humanity astounds me. What do you do, save it for your photos? Oh, wait, it's not in *those* either . . ."

"Oh, fuck off, you digital dork. God, I'm not going to miss you."

Culler points to me. "Her dad just died."

"And Eddie should know my loathing of you does not extend to her father or her."

"You call an unoriginal photographer unoriginal just *once*," Culler tells me, "and they never, ever get over it."

"Uhm, where are his things?" I have no idea what I've walked into.

She points behind me. I turn. Against the back wall, underneath the window, is a single, medium-size cardboard box, taped and sealed shut. I don't know how I keep it together enough to walk over to it. I bite my lip so hard I taste blood. I try to swallow it; I can't.

My legs feel like they're made of nothing. There has to be more than this.

He wouldn't just leave us with nothing.

I face her. "Is this it? Did you pack his things?"

"You packed his things?" Culler demands. "What the fuck right of that was yours?"

"I didn't *touch* his fucking things. That's what he left."

"Where's the rest of it?"

"There is no rest of it," Maggie says. "He got rid of it and left that box, which has been sitting there forever."

I turn to Culler. "When did he get rid of everything?"

He looks totally lost. "I wasn't here the week he . . . it had to be then, because the week before that . . ." He faces Maggie. "When did he get rid of everything?"

"I don't know."

"What *do* you know, Maggie? Anything?"

"How hard is it to pick up a box and *leave*?" She closes her magazine and gets to her feet. "I didn't touch his fucking things, Jesus. I didn't pack that box. I don't know when he got rid of it. I'm leaving. I'll be gone for an hour, Culler, and if you're here when I get back—"

Her voice fades out. Culler starts talking, but he sounds so far away, I can't get a handle on it. I stare at the box and run my hands over the cardboard. Do you know what this means? I want to ask them that. *Do you know what this means?*

The front door slams shut and it's quiet.

Maggie's gone.

She wouldn't care what it meant.

I press my hands against my eyes and exhale slowly. Culler's footsteps echo through the room as he walks over to me, stands close. He says my name, but if I move my hands I'll cry. I don't want to cry in front of Culler. I want to be cool and unflappable. I want to handle this. I have to handle this. I'm supposed to handle this. Beth sent me down here to handle this.

I am apparently the only person left who can handle this.

"Eddie," Culler says.

I move away from him and lower my hands and I don't cry, thank God, but I don't say anything either. Everything I'm feeling is so beyond anything I could say. When I finally do find the words, they fall out of my mouth, my voice breaking. Stupid and confused.

"So he knew he was going to do it for at least a week," I say. "So there were a few days where he was at home and he knew he was going to kill himself, which means he had time—"

I stop. I can't.

"Had time for what?" Culler asks.

"To leave behind something more," I mumble. "Better."

Sometimes I feel hunted by my grief. It circles me, stalks me. It's always in my periphery. Sometimes I can fake it out. Sometimes I make myself go so still, it can't sense that I'm there anymore and it goes away. I do that right now.

I go so still the thing inside me doesn't know I'm there anymore.

"Eddie?" Culler asks quietly.

I grab the box, but my hands quit on me, my dead hands, and it slips through my fingers and hits the floor. I hear the unmistakable sound of glass breaking and I start apologizing to no one, trying to pick it up again, but I can't.

I can't get my hands to work because they're too cold.

"Sorry." I can't grip the box. "I didn't—it's my hands. They're fucked up—"

"It's okay." Culler nudges me aside and picks up the box. "I've got it."

"Okay," I say. "Thank you."

He nods and I follow him through the door, outside. We put the box into the back of the station wagon without a word and seeing it there, by itself, makes me almost cry again, but I don't.

"Why are your hands fucked up?" Culler asks.

It's an empty and painful moment. It is the kind of moment that has me by the throat, the heart. Culler stands there and watches me and doesn't say anything.

"It's a long story," I finally answer.

"I've got the time."

"I don't really want to tell it."

"Well, that's too bad," he says.

"Why?"

He smiles ruefully. "Because now the only thing left for me to do is take you home."

uller has to take photographs of the studio before we leave. He catches me in one of them. I hold up my hands—delayed reaction—and tell him not to.

"Why not?" he asks. "You're beautiful."

"You're full of it," I say, and then I realize it sounds like I'm fishing for compliments and I don't want him to think that. "I mean—thank you."

No one has ever called me beautiful before and I'm surprised by how strange and uncomfortable it makes me feel. It's not a word I've ever considered for myself—or thought that other people would either, I guess.

"You're welcome," he says.

In the car, we're quiet. I don't know what to say. The box in the backseat makes the silence too heavy to breathe around and I ask Culler if I can open the window. He tells me sure and I roll it all the way down. The wind rushing into the car drowns out the sound of the radio, the sound of my heart beating. The box is still in the backseat, though.

I roll up the window and the silence is immediate. The box, the box. I tuck my hair behind my ears—Beth is right, I really need to cut it—and then I rub my eyes and rest my head against the seat. The box. I close my eyes.

Stop thinking about it.

"You have so many of his mannerisms," Culler says suddenly. "You move the same way he did. You speak—the way you say certain words, it's exactly on . . ."

"Does that freak you out?" I ask.

"No."

It freaks me out, a little. I am so much my father. I know this. People used to tell me that all the time. I have his hands, his face—the same fine features, brown eyes, and thick brown hair. By the time I started looking like he did when he was my age, strangers were mistaking him for my grandfather. I wonder if that ever bothered him, being so much older than my mom, older than other fathers who had seventeen-year-old daughters. Like, if every time he looked at me, he felt his age and how much closer that made him to death than he used to be, like Beth does, but not like Beth exactly. I wonder if that would be a reason to kill yourself.

Maybe that's why he killed himself.

It's so quiet. Being quiet with Culler isn't the same as being quiet with Milo. It doesn't feel like something important is missing.

We're about halfway back to Branford—floating through this town called Corby—when Culler says he has two cases of beer in the back of the station wagon, under the seat. He suggests we make a toast to my father and I agree, even though I hate the taste of beer. I just want to spend more time with him. I don't want to go home.

Corby is nice. Culler drives us to this Catholic high school, St. Peter's, and parks sideways in the parking lot. We sit on the pavement, behind the car, our backs against it, out of sight of any passersby. It feels wrong and right at the same time. Summer vacation looks great on schools. I'm dreading senior year.

I glance at Culler. He's taking the caps off the bottles with his teeth, which is vaguely impressive. He's so past high school. He must think I'm a little kid. He passes me a bottle.

Or maybe not.

"To Seth," he says.

"My dad."

We clink bottles and swig the beer in unison. It's warm. Gross.

"The last time I was at that studio . . ." He trails off and takes another swig from his bottle. I wonder if the objective is to be drunk and stuck here until we sober up. "The last time I was at that studio . . . he had contact sheets, negatives, equipment—and he just . . . got rid of it."

"Did you want it?" I ask. "I would've let you have it." It's out of my mouth before I know if I mean it, but then I decide that I mean it. If my dad had left it all behind, I would have let Culler take what he wanted. "I'm sorry."

"No," he says. He gives me a small smile. "Don't be. That's very sweet."

He thinks I'm a little kid.

I finish off the beer and wait to feel something, but I don't feel anything except sort of tired and sad. Culler doesn't touch his beer and it's more than half full and I think that means it's time to go, but I don't want to leave just yet.

I don't want to go home.

"What's with you and Maggie?" I ask.

"You don't want to know."

"Try me," I say.

"We had a thing . . ."

"A thing?" I repeat, and then he looks at me and I feel my face turn totally red and he laughs again and I wish I'd kept my mouth shut. "Oh God . . . *Maggie?*" And then I make it even worse: "She doesn't seem like . . ."

"Oh, I know," Culler says. "I know. I mean, it was okay, I guess." He shrugs. "She got to the point where she wanted to know what I really thought of her work and I felt like it would be okay to tell her."

I cringe. "Honesty is not the best policy?"

"She's very unoriginal."

"She's fairly well-known."

"Most unoriginal people are."

"Does that mean my father was unoriginal?"

"No. Besides, by the time he died, he wasn't that well-known." He pauses and laughs again, looking away from me like I've unnerved him a little. "I'm just talking." He runs his hand through his hair. "Should we go?"

I don't want to go back. I don't. The idea of going back makes me feel so sick, now that I'm so far from home. And then I have this crazy vision of Culler and me traveling so far away together. It's insane but I'm desperate not to go back to Mom, to Beth, to Milo. I search for something to say and there's nothing. My eyes travel to the station wagon.

The box inside.

I glance at Culler. He stares up at the sky and then stands and my heart jumps. I grab his leg without thinking and before he can ask me what's going on, I say, "I wonder what he thought was worth leaving behind."

Culler looks at me. "You want to open the box?"

At first, I thought I'd wait until I was alone to open it because it's private, but I'd never get that moment. Beth would be on me from the minute I brought it into the house and who knows how Mom would deal with it. Not that this truly matters, since I'm just using it as an excuse to stay longer. Still. Culler is probably the best person to do this with. Logically.

"Yeah," I say. "If you'll—if you want to . . ."

"I'd be honored," he says, and then his face reddens when he realizes how formal it sounds coming out of his mouth. "I mean it, though. I would be."

He holds out his hand and helps me to my feet. We stand there for a second, staring at the box, and my heart pounds and I realize how big this is and how I used it, just so I could spend more time with Culler.

Now I feel really sick.

But I pretend like it's nothing I can't handle. I open the door and pull the box out and my hands hang on tight this time. Glass clinks inside and I don't want to think about what I broke, but I'll know in a second.

I set the box on the pavement and we stare at it. The seams are taped perfectly, and my skin crawls at the idea of him taping this up, knowing the whole time he would kill himself and I would come here and find it. Anger wells up inside me, turns my blood hot. He knew. Of course he knew. Duh. But I feel dumb because some part of me was pretending his death was something he committed to on the spur of the moment. Not an intention he kept with him, close to his heart, while he was with us.

Acting like everything was fine.

I bend down and dig at the tape but my fingernails are useless against it. Culler bends down beside me and he has a Swiss Army knife attached to his car keys. He runs it down the middle of the tape, cutting a perfect line. The cardboard releases its hold. A sharp little sound. He steps back and waits for me to open it. I will open it. I'll open it. I open it.

I pull the cardboard flaps aside and stare into the box.

The edges of six frames stare up at us.

Six photographs.

Culler and I look at each other. I sit down and he sits next to me and I pull the first frame out and the next, and the next, and the next. The fifth one is the one I broke. I want to pick the ragged glass edges out of the black border but I don't. I lay them all out, until we're surrounded.

The photographs are of six locations. All black-and-white. I only recognize one of them—Tarver's. It's the third photograph I set out. It was taken at night and the building looks like it's glowing, and I don't even know how that's possible because there are no lights at Tarver's.

The stars are all behind it.

For a second, I can feel myself up on the roof. At night. I can feel it like I'm in the photograph. My head spins a little. I close my eyes for a second and then I open them again.

"Tarver's," Culler says, following my gaze. He points to the first photograph I set out, a run-down-looking barn. "That's an abandoned barn . . . I was there when he took that one . . ." He points to the third photograph I set out: an empty house. The doors and windows are boarded up. "I was there for that one too."

He skips over Tarver's and goes straight to the fourth photograph. It's of a beaten, falling-apart gazebo in the middle of a field. He shakes his head.

"But not that one." He moves on to the next. "That's an old, abandoned one-room schoolhouse. I was with him for that one too . . ." And then there is the last photo. A worn-down, tired-looking church. "Not that one."

He leans back and takes a longer look at them, totally awed in a way I am just not comprehending.

"Jesus," he says quietly. "These are the last photographs he worked on . . ."

He's thinking that's amazing and I am thinking:

These are what my dad thought was worth leaving behind and they are nothing.

"You should have them," I say abruptly.

Culler's head jerks up. "What?"

I grab the photos and start putting them back in the box. I want to throw them, but I don't. I'm shaking. "You should have them. They mean something to you. I don't get art, really, so I want you to have them—"

"Eddie—"

"No, I'm serious." My eyes burn. "I want you to have them, Culler."

"Eddie—"

"Just say you'll take them," I snap, and then I feel bad. "Sorry."

"I'll take them," he says. I move to get up, but I can't. I press my palms into the concrete and I feel his eyes on me. "Eddie . . . what were you expecting?"

The question takes it out of me and I feel tiredness seeping into my bones from no place I can source. Nothing is right.

"More," I say.

Culler moves closer to me. "I'm sorry."

"You know what his note said? It said he had to leave." My voice breaks. I swallow hard. "That's it. That's so much nothing." I gesture to the box. "And those—aren't even great photographs. They're nothing too."

And then I feel really bad for saying that.

"Eddie," Culler says. He reaches out and presses his hands against my face. Our eyes meet. "Do you really want me to have the photographs?"

"Take them. They don't mean anything to me," I say. "They don't mean . . . anything . . . I thought . . ." I shake my head. God, I'm going to cry. "I thought they'd mean something—tell me . . ." And then I do start to cry and I can't stop. "I needed it to."

Our eyes meet and something changes. Something changes in him. I feel it through his hands against my face, like everything inside him stops. And then starts again.

He brushes my tears away with his thumbs.

"It's okay," he says, but it's not okay. "Eddie, it's okay. I understand."

He leans forward and kisses me.

It's not just a kiss. His lips are insistent, searching, trying to get the feel of me, and my heart is so heavy and sad. I feel that from him too. This is a funeral kiss. This is a kiss for the dead. We miss my father too much for it to mean more. But it's still the nicest thing that's happened to me lately. He feels warm. His tongue is in my mouth.

I think the dumbest thing: *I would take off all my clothes for you.*

It's so dumb, but it's the thought his mouth on my mouth puts into my head.

And when he pulls away, I say the dumbest thing: "I'm seventeen."

He laughs.

We don't talk a lot on the way back to Branford. I'm glad because I'm not sure I could trust myself to speak. By the time he drops me back off at Fuller's, long after Milo's shift has ended, we say goodbye like nothing happened.

turn on the computer. I open up a browser and search Culler's name in Google. His site is the first hit. I don't know why I didn't do this before, when we were in the car together, because then I would've told him how much I admired his work even if I didn't really, because maybe then he would have kissed me twice. His site loads quickly. The first page is just his name in small black letters against a white background. It doesn't even say he's a photographer.

CULLER EVANS

I click through to the next page, which holds his artist's statement, but no photos yet. I feel like I'm reading a diary entry. It's what Culler told me in the car but more intimate, somehow. Personal.

ART IS NOT COMPROMISE. IT'S EVOLUTION—A COMBINATION OF BOLD TRUTHS AND LIES THAT YOU MUST BE BRAVE ENOUGH TO LOOK AT AND BRAVE ENOUGH TO SHARE . . . I BELIEVE IN ART AT ALL COSTS . . .

I stare at it for a long time before clicking SELECTED PHOTO-GRAPHS.

I am not a great judge of art. I honestly don't know what it is, or if it can be so defined, but these photographs are raw and strange. They begin and end, sad stories. All of them are sad and I wish he was here, so I could ask him about them. Ask him if it means he's sad.

There's one set of photos, a collection of a woman in a hospital bed that seems boring at first, nothing, until the final page, which turns all the photographs into an animation and you can see that the person is slowly exhaling. He's titled it *Last Breath* and I'm afraid it means what I think it does and then I can't stop looking, because if this woman is not dying, I've decided she is. That makes me feel really weird.

Another series, *Compassion*, follows a beautiful woman (girl-friend? I hope not) from a distance. He's shadowing her. She doesn't know he's there. I get absorbed in the story of her day as she moves from place to place, until the last photo is of her lying in an alley-way. In the corner of the photo, a shadowy figure retreats. I pause, my breath all caught in my throat.

That can't be real. Is it?

I end up questioning all of his photographs this way. They're narratives, definitely. They have beginnings, middles, and ends. They're all unsettling and private, but the strangest and most compelling thing about them is some of them—a lot of them—I can't tell if they're staged.

The angles he uses remind me of eavesdropping.

There is a series of a couple fighting in a kitchen. It's told backwards, from the end of the fight—she is walking away—to the beginning—they're smiling and laughing together. Culler calls that one *Best Friends*. A woman hitting her child in a store, first alone, and then by the last photo there's an audience and some of them look like they're enjoying watching it.

Culler calls that set *Perfect Day*.

Various photographs of people seen in ways no one wants to be seen. And there's a passiveness about them too—I should be inspired to act, but like the person behind the camera, all I can do is watch. I don't know how it makes me feel. One of the last sets is of a faceless couple totally fucking, which makes me feel weird. I think I like it. But that angle—I don't know if they know they're being photographed. The series is called *Apologies*.

I want to ask him what that even means.

I click away from the screen and lean back in my chair.

Something about Culler's kiss has made me so restless.

I keep replaying it in my mind—just the kiss—and then I take it one further. I imagine us having sex on the pavement and it's amazing. I think of it close. The way I see it in my head, it's all skin and touching and expert hands. And then my brain pans out and we're surrounded by all the photographs my father took. And that is when I stop replaying it in my mind.

For a couple of minutes.

I'm not restless enough to call Milo, who I also think of and imagine having sex with Missy because I'm a freak, but restless enough that when Beth starts pressing the haircut thing again, I say, "Fine. Let's go. Right now."

We're in the kitchen. Mom is upstairs in bed, where she's been for the last five days. That's not normal. This is a bad week because for all of the planning my dad apparently put into jumping off a building, he forgot their wedding anniversary would be the first post-death event. It's still not for another couple of weeks, but Mom looked at the calendar and saw it penciled in and it was all over from there.

I overheard her crying about it with Beth the night I got back from the studio. First she wanted to know if he remembered their anniversary and killed himself anyway. Then she wanted to know if he

was so full of the idea of dying, he just totally forgot. Then she realized neither was the better option and it all ended with her crawl-
ing into bed.

I stood outside the door to her bedroom, wanting to go in and
say something, but all I could think about was how much I hated
my dad for doing this to us and then I felt so sick and then Beth
came out and said, "Where did you put everything from the studio?"
I told her he'd gotten rid of it, all of it, and she relaxed and actually
said, "Oh, good. That makes it easier."

And then *I* crawled into bed.

Which is also when I started thinking about having sex with
Culler.

I want to have sex with someone.

What is wrong with me.

Beth and I maintain stony silence in the car. Well, I do. She
hums to herself—no radio, because it distracts her—and babbles
about what kind of cut I should get.

"You have well-defined cheekbones and sharp features," she
says. "I'll leave it up to Cory, but if you're going to keep it long, the
least you could do is ask him to thin it out, so it doesn't bushel
around your head."

Bushel around my *head*? I hate everything that comes out of this
woman's mouth. I study Beth. Her blond hair—which is already
going gray, but dyed to hide it—is cropped tight to her head and
she has such an ugly mouth. She has these tiny lips that she somehow turns into red colored squares with lipstick.

"I want to look like Marilyn Monroe," I tell her.

She laughs. "You're no Marilyn Monroe."

The hair salon is just off the mall and it's called CUTZ, which
makes me embarrassed for it, but it's a nice little place, I guess.
It's all yellow and checkered floors, which clashes horribly with the
country music they pipe in through the speakers.

Beth is really weird with me when we're out in public. She tries
to pretend we like each other or at the very least, *she* likes *me* and she

doesn't know what the fuck my problem is. She knows Cory, the stylist—an older man with frosted tips, which makes me feel embarrassed for him—and insists he be the one who cuts my hair. She tells him I'm the daughter of one of her oldest and dearest friends and he mouths, *the jumper?* when he thinks I'm not looking.

She nods and takes a seat in the waiting area.

Cory takes me to the back and washes my hair.

"So what kind of look are you after?" he asks over the water, and I feel really gross for liking how his old-man hands feel massaging my scalp.

"I don't know," I tell him. "Marilyn Monroe."

He laughs. Why does everyone think that's a joke? He finishes up and takes me back out front. The chair he puts me in is in front of three mirrors and next to the windows, so everyone can look in and see. I hate that. It's like being put on display.

"Have you always kept it long?" he asks, drawing my wet hair back with his hands. My hair stops just in the middle of my back. It always has. I nod.

Beth looks up from the gossip rag she's reading. "Doesn't the length drag her face down? No wonder you're always so sullen looking, Eddie."

"You look ready for a change," Cory tells me.

"Cut it all off," I say. I imagine myself bald. Shaved head. I almost say that but think better of it. "I mean—short but long. I mean, just different. But short. But long."

Beth gives Cory a wry look. "Did you get all that?"

Cory ties up my hair into a ponytail. My palms start to sweat. I wipe them on my pants. He notices and says, "Relax. This won't hurt a bit."

He grabs the scissors.

I catch sight of myself in the mirror and realize my father will never see me like this. I am becoming a person my father will never get to know. I am trying to force that thought out of my head at the same time Cory cuts the ponytail off. Just like that. Before I've even had time to prepare, to change my mind, it's gone and I'm that person *now*.

I dig my fingernails into the arm of my chair.

"Hey, kid—are you okay?" Cory says, noticing. "Beth—"

"What's the problem?" Beth is beside me before I can blink. She takes one look at my face and says, "Eddie, what's wrong with you?"

I'm not ready to be that person now.

Beth is convinced I have diabetes or hypoglycemia or something because I went all "rigid and strange" while Cory was cutting my hair.

She won't fucking leave it alone.

"My first thought was *it's her sugars*," Beth tells Mom over lunch, which consists of scary green smoothies for both of them and me sitting there and not eating anything. Now that Mom's out of bed, I want to be in the house less, but Milo hasn't called me and I know it's because if I said a fight was on, I have to tell him when it's off, but secretly I think he should end it because everyone's daily goal should be making things easier for me while I'm in mourning. "Does your family have a history of diabetes or anything like that?"

"What?" Mom asks. She's been staring out the window.

"And she's pale all the time," Beth continues. "Look at her— sallow, even. I can see it now that her hair is finally out of her face."

Mom stares at my hair for a long time, until she finally spots the difference.

"It's a nice haircut, Eddie," she says.

Beth frowns. "But look at her complexion. So pale."

"Maybe I need more Vitamin D," I suggest.

"Well, I've been saying *that* forever—"

"So I'll get some." I get to my feet. "Like, right now. I'll get some."

"Are you going out?" Mom asks. Something about this much of her voice after a forever of almost total silence is setting me on edge. "With Milo? I never see Milo around anymore . . ."

"When would you even notice that?" I ask.

It doesn't even come out of my mouth meanly, even though that's what I feel in my heart, but because she's my mother, she senses it. She knows where my heart is when I say it.

And she cries.

I leave the room awkwardly, my chest winding itself tight. Hearing your mother cry never gets easier to take. It's a sound that goes through you each time. I'd never seen her cry before he died. I'd never made her cry. I have made her cry. I push through the front door. I'm halfway down the walk when Beth appears.

"I got her to promise to *try* today," she says, furious. "She was trying and you *ruined* it."

It's the meanest thing Beth has ever said to me.

She goes back inside before I can say something equally mean to her.

Hate her. Hate this. Hate this. Hate this. I hate this. I grab my bike and pedal fast, hard. I focus on the way it feels, the air against my face. I'm going to tell Milo about this and then we will go to the river and he will have his flask and I will hate Beth and drink until I love the world again and everything in it.

But when I get to Fuller's, Missy's car is there. Of course.

I do a few laps in the parking lot next to Fuller's and debate going somewhere else, but fuck it. She can be his girlfriend all she wants. He was my friend first. And even if she *is* his girlfriend again, she's only here for the summer. Totally still a temp.

I pedal over, toss my bike on the ground, and practically throw myself inside, saying, "So! What are we all doing today?"

Missy and Milo are at the register, forever, always. They're surprised to see me.

Missy's eyes widen.

"You cut your hair!" She rushes over and pulls at the ends. "Oh, wow, Eddie. That looks great. You can totally see your face."

"Nice face," Milo says behind her.

Missy keeps touching it. Cory did an okay job on my hair, I guess, after my freak-out. He thinned it out and made it short—just barely past my chin—with jagged edges and declared it a style. I can live with it. I mean, it could have been worse. In a place like CUTZ, I could've just as easily walked out with some kind of country music–inspired disaster.

"Thanks," I mutter, moving away from Missy.

Nobody says anything. I look at Milo and he looks at me, but he's not giving me an out or any help. It makes me mad. I don't want to talk to him with her here.

So I don't say anything.

But Missy eventually catches on and she says, "Oh, hey. You know what? I told my grandpa I'd pick up a bag of mulch from the co-op for him. I should do that while I remember. Be right back."

"See you in a few," Milo says.

She leaves.

Milo turns back to the register like he finds it very interesting.

I lean against one of the freezers.

Silence.

"We're not in a fight anymore," I finally tell him.

"I'm thrilled," he says.

It comes out of his mouth casually, but he hates me when he says it, like I hated my mom when I spoke to her earlier and I don't know what upsets me more, me doing that to her or him doing that to me but I feel it all on me and my face gives it away.

"Shit," he says, alarmed. "Eddie, I'm—"

"Don't," I tell him. "Forget it."

No sign of Missy yet. My father is dead. He killed himself. The studio is cleaned out. I have been kissed by a guy who is older than me and knows how to kiss. I've been thinking about how I want to have sex. I cut my hair. My mom tried to talk to me today and I ruined it. Beth says I ruined it. This whole summer is a bust.

"How did cleaning out the studio go?" Milo asks. I shrug. If he wanted to know, he could've taken me. "Who was that guy? The one that drove you? That wasn't Beth."

I don't know why I like that Milo wants to know, but I like it. I like it in a weird way I shouldn't. It makes me tingle a little bit.

"Beth uhm, bailed. He's a photographer. A student. My father's student," I answer. Milo raises an eyebrow. "I know. I didn't know about him before . . . He gave me a ride and helped me clear out everything. His name is Culler Evans."

"How old is he?"

"Twenty-one," I lie. I don't know why. "He's nice."

"It was nice of him to help you."

"Yeah."

"I really wish I could have—"

"I was serious, though," I interrupt, because I don't want to hear it from him. I want to hear it less and less. "What are we doing today?"

"You actually want to hang out with us?" Milo asks. "Because if you do, we're going to Jenna's after my shift. Jenna and Aaron, me, you, Missy. Wasting an afternoon around the pool. Sound good?"

I nod, but I wonder if he really wants me there. It's probably easier for everyone when I'm not around.

He would freak if I said that out loud.

Jenna's been popular ever since she got a pool, which was the sixth grade. It's not one of those lame, aboveground pools either. Inground. Great length. It's cool. We all flock to it and we never stop being impressed by it because rural life means being that easy. I think the nicest thing about lounging around Jenna's pool is that you can be present, but you don't have to engage and by not engaging, you're engaging. Disengaging is engaging.

I drink a couple of beers with Missy and end up dozing on a towel next to the pool. Jenna's loaned me one of her swimsuits. All she seems to own are bikinis.

Maybe I'll get a tan.

But it's awesome that this is all I have to do. It's enough. Conversations happen around me and sometimes I'll chime in or laugh when someone's said something funny, but mostly I just enjoy the lack of expectations and the sun on my face.

This is how my summer was supposed to be.

"Hey." Milo pokes me in the side. He's been sitting next to me, his legs in the pool, for the last hour or so. "Switch sides or you'll burn."

"I always burn," I tell him, but I roll onto my stomach and turn my head to the pool. Missy and Jenna are at the other end, talking and pretending to watch Aaron dive. He takes it really seriously, which is funny because it's not like he's on any teams or anything. It's not like Branford High even has a pool. I close my eyes again.

I wonder what Culler Evans is doing right now.

"Sunscreen?" Milo asks.

"I guess."

I expect him to hand me the bottle but he doesn't. Just like that, his hands are on my back, smoothing the lotion into my skin, and I tense because it's the freakiest thing.

"My mom tried today," I tell him.

"That's great."

He sounds like he means it.

"I made her cry."

"That's not so great."

He pushes what's left of my hair back from my neck, and I feel him hesitate, just for a second. Noticing the difference. I wonder what he really thinks of it and if he likes it or if he doesn't. I wonder if I care either way.

At what point is sunscreen fully absorbed into the skin? Milo touches me longer than he has to, but that's okay. His palms smooth across my shoulder blades. I keep my eyes closed. After a while, his hands are off me, but I feel that he's near, more than I did before. For some reason it makes me feel sad but grateful. I want to open my eyes and tell him it's nice to know that he's there, but I don't. I just want to keep this moment going as long as I can.

And because that's what I want, of *course* Missy swims over and ruins it.

"Getting in?" she asks him.

"Nah," he says. "It's nice out here."

"It's nice in here too."

I almost risk cracking an eye open just to see what kind of look they're exchanging when Aaron's voice drifts from the other side of the pool.

"Ready for this?" he calls.

"Aaron, you asshole, get down from there," Missy yells. "You'll break your neck."

I open my eyes. Missy and Milo are turned away from me. It takes me a minute to spot Aaron. I look to the diving board first, but he's not there.

He's on the roof.

He climbed out there through Jenna's window. The visual makes my heart jump, spastic beats, horrible beats—an ugly fear running through my veins even though I know it's not what it looks like. Aaron is going to jump off the roof and into the pool. The ultimate dive. It's stupid and it's dangerous, but it's not impossible. I've seen this happen at Jenna's house before.

No one has ever died doing it.

"I'm fine," Aaron shouts.

"He's fine," Jenna echoes. "He's done this a hundred times."

Missy and Milo are quiet, eyes trained on Aaron, and before

anyone can blink, Aaron launches himself off the roof and the time it takes him to fall seems like one of those forever kind of seconds—the kind you feel every inch of yourself present for, the kind where you can absorb every detail and recall it easily later, but also the kind that's gone so quickly you wonder how it's even possible to have walked away with that much of it carved into your soul.

He hits the water with a loud splash. I flinch.

And then it's over.

But some things—they just ruin your day.

Like, completely.

"Asshole," Milo mutters. His voice is strained. I close my eyes. "She see it?"

"No," Missy says. There are wet splashy sounds and I realize Missy is hoisting herself out of the pool. I imagine how jiggly that must look; she's in a bikini too. "I'm going in to get a beer. Come with me."

"Sure," Milo says. He reaches over and squeezes my shoulder. His hands are trembling. I shrug him off because I can't stand how that feels. It doesn't feel nice, his touching me—not like before. He leans close to my ear. "Hey, wake up. We're going inside for a second. Coming?"

"No," I say.

"You want anything?"

"No."

He squeezes my shoulder again and then they go. I lay there for a minute and then I open my eyes. Aaron is doing laps around the pool. He really is an asshole, but it's not his fault, I guess. It's not like my dad died so he can never jump off roofs in front of me again.

"What's the roof feel like?" I ask, when he gets close to me.

He pauses and treads water. His black hair is plastered against his forehead. He pinches his nose and says, "It's sort of hot. Makes sense, though, right? Closer to the sun."

"Were you afraid?"

"I've done it before."

"You could bash your head off the side of the pool. Brains everywhere," I say, and he lets out a nervous laugh. "How can you be sure that's not going to happen?"

"It's really not that far," Aaron says, gesturing to the roof. Jenna's window is wide open, where he climbed out. The roof slopes down, closer to the pool than it isn't. "Just get a little momentum and you're good." He studies me. "Gonna do it?"

"Jump off a roof?" I ask. "You mean, like my dad?"

Aaron's eyes get round, but he doesn't say anything. I get to my feet and pad across the hot concrete. I pull open the sliding glass doors that lead into the kitchen. Missy, Jenna, and Milo are gathered around the island. I spot limeade, tequila and beer. Missy catches my eye.

"Beer margaritas," she explains. "Want one?"

I make a face. "No, thanks."

"Good call," Milo says.

"Shut up, they taste awesome," Jenna says.

I pass them and make my way into the living room.

"Where are you going?" Milo calls after me.

"Gotta pee," I call back.

"That's what the pool's for," he says.

Jenna and Missy break into a chorus of *ewwws* and giggles.

I walk up the stairs. My stomach is twisting and my palms are sweaty-nervous because I'm going to climb out that window and I am going to jump into the pool. I imagine this walk for my father. The way to Tarver's. He probably wasn't nervous. He was so ready. How do you get to a point where you're that ready?

Will I reach it by the time I reach the window?

Jenna's bedroom is all purple. It's very Jenna. The window is wide open, and a feeble breeze is pushing the sheer white curtains my way. They're hands, reaching out to me. I go to them. I have my foot on the sill. I'm halfway out. I can see the pool from here.

I can't tell if I'm afraid I'll jump or I'm afraid I won't.

What if I'm that statistic that hits the concrete even though the water is so close?

"Don't." Milo's voice is behind me, but I don't turn around. "Eddie, if you do I'll never speak to you again."

"There's water," I say. "I'm not suicidal."

"I mean it."

"Aaron looked like he was having fun." I stare out. It's a longer drop than from my bedroom window. It's the highest up I've ever been. "Do you think the answer is in the fall?"

"Eddie, shut up."

I force myself through the window and stand straight up on the roof. It's dizzying for a second. If I lost my footing, I would miss, maybe. Or not miss.

"Eddie."

"I want to go up on the roof at Tarver's," I tell him, glancing back. He's at the window and he looks mad. "But I'm too scared. I want you to go with me."

"I won't go there with you."

"Why?"

"Because there's nothing there," he says impatiently. "Get back inside. You'll get hurt."

"Aaron jumped and he didn't get hurt."

"Aaron does it all the time and he's just doing it for fun—"

I turn around. Too fast. I overbalance and grab on to the sill to steady myself. Milo grabs my arm. I'm bent over and our faces are close.

"What do you think I'm trying to do?" I ask.

"You play chicken with trucks and wander around condemnable buildings at night," he says. "I have no idea what you're trying to do."

"Liar," I say.

He stares at me for a long minute.

"None of this is going to tell you anything," he finally says.

It's like my heart dissolves into a million angry bubbles that find their way up my throat. He gets it, but he doesn't, and that's worse. I want to tell him I'll know what it's like to really fall and that's something I wouldn't have known yesterday. That's important.

"I'm going to do it."

His grip moves from my arm. He grabs my hand, wrapping his fingers around my fingers. He squeezes them.

"Your hand is cold," he says.

I hesitate. "I told you."

"Eddie, please come back inside."

He looks at me in a way that breaks my heart, like I'm hurting him. He pulls me back into Jenna's bedroom and I let him. He keeps his fingers around mine and we sit on the bed, holding hands.

"You were there, Milo," I say. "Tell me."

"Eddie, I don't know why he killed himself."

"You were still there," I say, "and you won't talk about it."

"You were there too. I don't need to."

"You make me feel alone."

I can't believe I just say it like that. *You make me feel alone.* Maybe I confuse him. Maybe he doesn't know when what happened stops being about my dad and starts being about us. It confuses me too.

"I'm sorry." He says it so quietly. He squeezes my hand. "Feel that?"

"They're not numb," I mumble. "Just cold."

He exhales slowly and then he stares at the ceiling.

"They're not cold," he says. ". . . They were cold."

I look at him.

"I called your cell that night," he says, and my breath catches in my throat. He looks at me and his eyes are completely defeated. "And you didn't pick up. It felt different."

Like the world changed. That's what I want to say, but I don't. The same thing that made him call me was the same thing that made me go to my father, when I'd never done that before.

It felt different.

"I called your house and your mom told me you were at Tarver's." He falls silent for a minute. "I don't know why I went . . ."

Downstairs, I can hear Missy and Jenna laughing. Aaron's voice. It's all so out of place. They are. We are. I don't know anymore. Nothing is right in this moment, even though I think I'm finally getting what I want.

"I don't remember hearing my phone," I say suddenly. I can't remember hearing my phone but I know it was with me. "At all . . ."

"I wish you had," he says. "When I—"

He breaks off. Stops. I wait. Maybe he needs a minute and I'll let him have the minute, but then the minute passes and he shakes his head and says, "I can't," and gets up from the bed, his hand free of my hand. It feels so empty.

"Just get it over with," I tell him.

"No—"

"Milo—"

"Just fucking *stop*, Eddie!" he pleads. I close my eyes and then he says, "I'm sorry." He clears his throat. "Look, I'm going back downstairs, so if you—"

"Whatever."

"Eddie—"

"Forget it."

I open my eyes.

He pauses. "You're not going to—"

"Just *go*." Asshole.

He goes. I stay in Jenna's room for a really long time. No one bothers me, which is weird. I wonder what Milo told them. If Jenna was hanging out in my room while everyone else was having a great time downstairs, I wouldn't be okay with that, even if you threw a recently deceased father into the mix. I wonder if that makes me a bad person.

And then I hear footsteps making their way down the hall.

I hope it's Milo, but it's not.

It's that other person whose name starts with M.

"Hey," Missy says. Her hair doesn't look that great post-pool. Stringy and dried out. It makes her face seem too round. This is one of those rare instances I look better than her.

"Hi," I say.

She sits down beside me. I bet Jenna sent her.

"Where's Milo?"

"Drinking in the garage with the guys," she says. "Deacon and Jeff are here."

"Oh."

"Are you okay?" Missy asks. I roll my eyes and then I feel like a jerk for doing it. Luckily, she laughs and says, "Stupid question."

"Yeah," I say.

Maybe it's not. Maybe I'm being unfair. A cool breeze is coming in through the open window. I stare outside, past the sloping roof. From the bed, you can only see the edge of the pool, and my towel, where I left it. The lighter part of this afternoon already feels far away.

I make things so awkward.

"I'm not jealous of you," I blurt out. She stares at me. "I mean, I'm not trying to make things really weird between all three of us. I don't hate you guys together or anything—"

"What?"

I feel my face turn red. I don't know how I can put it any more simply. Trust Marilyn Monroe to be stupid enough not to get it. Okay, that is unfair because I think I read somewhere Marilyn Monroe was smarter than anyone ever gave her credit for.

"Just . . ." I shrug. "That."

"Eddie," she says slowly, really uncomfortable now. I wish I'd kept my mouth shut. Why did I have to say that. "Eddie, Milo and I are totally not together like that."

My mind goes blank. "Yes, you are."

"No," she says. "Did he tell you that?"

"I—"

I try to remember every conversation I've had with Milo that's centered around Missy, but I can't. Not word for word. But I also can't remember him saying he was with her now.

But I also can't remember him denying it.

"I thought . . ."

My stomach sinks.

He made me think.

"I have a boyfriend," Missy says. "Milo and I are friends now. We just talk."

I don't know what to say. I feel so stupid and angry and worse, still jealous. *Milo and I are just friends*. What does he need Missy to be his *friend* for? They just talk—but he won't talk to me. This is worse than when I thought they were together. At least then I could understand *why* Missy was between us, if they were getting each other off, but now it isn't even that.

He goes to her. Not me.

"I'm his best friend," I say, before I can stop myself.

She looks so sad for me, I want to die.

"I know. Of course you are." Her voice is patronizing but her eyes are painfully sincere. "You mean, like, everything to him." I snort, because I don't believe that anymore. "No, I mean . . . when he told me about your dad and how he found you, it was like—"

Stop.

"He told you about that?"

"Yeah, but . . ."

That's it. That is so it. I get up. She reaches for me.

"Eddie, wait—"

I can't even look at her. I can't do this right now. I leave the room. I leave the house. I'm always leaving, but I never have anywhere to go.

Beth gives me the most disgusted look when I step through the door; I'm still in the bikini I borrowed from Jenna. That's a crime, I guess. She has one of those nature CDs on. It sounds like a thunderstorm. That is probably not a coincidence.

"Where's Mom?"

"She's upstairs."

"Surprise, surprise."

I find a glass from the cupboard and fill it with water, my back to Beth. I hope she's looking at me. I hope she's seeing how young I am, how perfect I am in all the right places while her skin is turning into one giant problem area. Cellulite and stretch marks and wrinkles.

"And whose fault is that?"

"What do you *want* from me?" I face her. "You don't want me here while you help her, so you tell me to leave. I leave. I come back and you give me shit—"

She slams her hand on the table and the sound makes me jump.

"I've had enough of your attitude! I'm not an idiot, Eddie. I know what you're thinking when you give me those *looks*. You don't want me here, that's *fine*. But I *am*. You could cooperate more. You could say *thank you*—"

"*You* could leave me *alone*—"

"I am *trying* to keep this household together!" She actually shrieks it and then she pinches the bridge of her nose and tries to collect herself. Cleansing breaths. "And that requires a certain level of organization. I need you to be present in some ways and absent in others so I can pull your mother out of this and then we'll deal with what's left—"

"You mean me," I interrupt.

"Your mother needs it *now*," she snaps, and my heart stops because I think she just told me my pain was less than my mother's, but I cannot get my mouth to move to ask her. "Don't look at me like that, Eddie. I don't understand where you're coming from half of the time—"

"Side effect of aging," I suggest.

"Why can't you just be mature about—"

"Maybe your brain cells are dying."

"You know, your father would hate that you're talking to me like this."

I see red. I *see* it. Everything goes red, a red door, and I throw the glass I'm holding into the sink. It breaks. It's not some spectacular shatter into a thousand pieces, it just goes into two pieces. The cracking sound it makes is so fucked up—how loud it is.

The quiet it creates.

"Would he?" I ask her, my voice trembling. "You think? Really?"

Beth starts to cry, and as cutting as the sound is when it comes out of my mother, it's so surprising, so awful coming from her. I want to ask her if she misses him too. But I can't.

I don't know what to do.

"*Go,*" she says. "Get out of my sight."

I go upstairs. I shut the door to my bedroom and sink down to the floor and my hands are shaking, cold. I pinch them. I can still feel them. Just cold. This is awful. This is so hopeless. We're all lost in different ways, so how do we even help each other find our way out. We won't. We can't. We'll just stay lost forever.

It's eleven when I get the text from Milo. This is the longest day of my life.

OUTSIDE. UNDER THE STREETLIGHT.

I text him back.

FUCK OFF.

I wait a minute, and then:

WALKED ALL THE WAY FROM J'S FOR YOU.
FUCK OFF.
YOU COULD'VE TOLD ME YOU WERE LEAVING.

I toss my phone on my bed. I'm wearing a tank top and underwear. I guess I should scale down the roof in more than that. I put on a pair of shorts, open the window, and climb over the sill. Déjà vu. It's been too long since I've been to Tarver's. Maybe I should try for the roof again. Maybe I'm strong enough to do it now, just from meeting Culler. The first time I went to Tarver's, I imagined there was something real on that roof. A reason. Answers.

I haven't been able to let that thought go.

I jump down. I land. I spot Milo under the streetlight across the road and feel really embarrassed about telling him to fuck off twice, about ditching him at Jenna's, because I have a feeling Missy probably freaked at him about it. When I reach him, I can smell pot and booze and he seems a little far away, but he's not wasted, though. I've seen Milo wasted.

"You could've told me you were leaving," he repeats.

"You could've told me Missy had a boyfriend back in Pikesville," I return. He has the decency to look embarrassed. "Why did you lie?"

"I don't know," he says, and I move to go back to the house but he grabs my arm. "I'm serious, Eddie. I don't know why I let you think that."

"And she said you told her what happened, that night at Tarver's, but you don't tell me." My voice breaks, already. Embarrassing, but these words are hard to say to him. "But you told *her* about it—"

"I just told her once—"

"So tell *me* once—"

"*Stop fucking asking!*—" Explosion. He's yelling at me. "Seriously. I don't know how many times I can tell you I don't want to talk about it before you get it!"

I take a step back and his eyes widen, like he can't believe he did that, but I can and that just makes it worse.

"I'm sorry," he says. "I didn't mean . . ."

But he did.

We stand apart from each other.

"I hate you," I tell him.

"No, you don't."

But he's so wrong. I hate him for this so much it hurts. I will hate him for this forever. It will fester between us until I can't stand to be around him, and maybe he'll finally tell me *then*, but it will be too late, because I'll never be able to forget this feeling. I'll never forget how he kept it from me and how bad that made me feel.

"You hate me," I say.

"No," he says. "Never . . ."

And then he stares past me, to my house.

"Remember that time I ran away?" he asks.

I do; instantly. It was the third grade. We can't remember what he was so mad about that he decided he'd Leave Branford and Show Them All anymore, but we both think it must've been stupid because it was the third grade.

"I hid out at your place," he says. "Your dad called my parents so they knew where I was. I told him I was leaving and I was taking you with me and he said it was fine, remember? And he asked you if that was okay, and you said it was and he said okay . . ."

I want to tell Milo the saddest part of remembering this is that I'm remembering my dad the way he looked now—older than he was then. In my head, his impending suicide shows over the face of the person he pretended to be. I think that means my memories of him are ruined.

"But later, when we were alone, you started bawling because you didn't want to leave your parents. So I told you to stay, and then you got even more upset—like it was the end of the world. You said you wouldn't let me go by myself. You wouldn't. You didn't." He pauses. "In the second grade, I felt like I got stuck with you . . . but . . . after that it was different."

I don't know what to say.

"And . . . then your dad died and it was . . . it was different again." He swallows. "Eddie, I don't know how I . . ."

I don't know what he's saying.

And then he kisses me.

He kisses me.

He brings his hand to my face and he kisses me, his mouth on mine, and I feel a door closing, something locking me in my head so all I can do is think things while it's happening. It's like my lips are dead and my brain is on, but it's short-circuiting. *My best friend mouth Missy hands cold dumb idiot second grade mouth Culler best friend Milo Milo Milo Milo Milo . . .*

His lips press against my lips and his palms lie gently against the side of my face. His hands are warm. My hands are cold. His hands move to my hair. I kiss him back and regain the ability to think in full sentences and I regret it immediately: *What does this mean? How can he kiss me? How can he kiss me? How can he kiss me? Oh my God, he's kissing me.*

It's too much.

I pull away at the same time I completely change my mind. I don't want it to stop and I almost bring my hands to him, to make him close to me again, but I think the moment is really over.

Did that happen? It didn't . . .

"Sorry," I blurt out. Why am I apologizing? He's the one who kissed me. I feel like I'm going to cry. Why does this make me want to cry. "I'm sorry—"

"It's okay," he says, and then he kisses me again and it is infinitely different from the first time, like all the years of our knowing each other are in this kiss and he would know how to kiss me just by knowing me . . . and I think *Culler* again but the thought is quieter—

But it's not quiet enough.

"Milo," I say against his mouth, and he kisses me again and gives me space enough to talk, but we're still so close our foreheads are touching. And now that I have space enough to talk, I don't know what to say. "I can't. I really—I can't—"

"It's okay," he says. "We can go back from this."

It comes out of his mouth so kind—he means it—and it just makes me feel worse. That he can kiss me like this and change everything, but still promise me nothing has to change because I can't promise him anything.

"It's not you—" Except it is. *But it's this other guy too.* But I'm smarter than saying that. *And oh, my father is dead. And you keep things from me that I need to know.*

"I know. I mean I understand," he says, and I start shaking my head and he says, "No really, I get it and it's fine. I'll see you tomorrow, okay? I'll see you . . ."

I press my lips together and nod.

"It's okay," he repeats. He grabs my hand and forces a smile at me. "Eddie, seriously. It's okay. Nothing has to be different."

I nod again, and then I stay there, under the streetlight, and watch him go.

I think Milo is becoming the biggest liar I know.

t's hard to sleep. It eventually happens and when I wake up again it's late, close to evening late. An entire day passed me by and I'm tired. I am still so tired.

My phone buzzes on my nightstand and I answer it without looking at the number because I'm sure—*so* sure—it's him.

"Milo?"

"No." My heart stops at the voice, the familiarity. I shiver; someone walking over my grave. A memory of a different kiss drifts into my head. "Will you meet me?"

Culler.

We decide to meet at Chester's.

When I ask him what time, he tells me he's ten minutes away and my stomach flips, nervous, excited. I was in bed, sleeping, and he was making his way to me that whole time.

That's amazing.

I change into jeans and a hoodie, even though it's too hot for a hoodie. Now I need an exit strategy. Mom and Beth are downstairs. The sun is dipping into the horizon and neither of them has seen me all day. Neither of them has come for me. I'm afraid I'll never forgive my mother for all the times she didn't come for me. But whatever.

I don't need to think about that now.

I go out the window and sneak away with my bike and more time slips by and I'm afraid he'll leave before I get there, but that's stupid. He came out all this way to see me.

I love that thought. It pushes every thought of Milo out of my head.

My heart beats funny when I get to Chester's. The place is busier than I've ever seen it and Culler's station wagon is parked at the far end of the lot. He's not in it, though. I wipe my palms on my jeans. I just want to be cool. Basically.

When I step inside, I'm met with a blast of cold air. Santo and Johnny's "Sleep Walk" is playing through the speakers and it's like I've walked into a movie or something. I spot Culler at the back of the room. He waves me over and I cut a path to him through the din of farmers eating and talking, imagining I can feel all of their eyes on me as I do.

"Who's Milo?" Culler asks as I sit across from him. He has a sloppy-looking canvas bag next to him. "Boyfriend?" Before I can answer, he says, "I hope you don't mind, but I ordered for you . . ."

I don't know which question to answer first, so instead I end up mumbling, "I'm sorry if I kept you waiting . . ."

"I didn't give you a lot of notice." He gestures to my face. "New haircut."

My face turns red. "Yeah."

"It really suits you," he says.

The waitress walks over then, with two Cokes and two plates of fries. She sets them in front of us and Culler actually looks kind of embarrassed.

"I figured nobody hates fries, right?"

"Oh, it's fine," I say. "Milo and I always get the cheese fries when . . ."

Or maybe: shut the fuck up, Eddie.

"Boyfriend?" Culler asks again.

"He's not my boyfriend," I say. I stare at the fries and try to imagine eating after saying that. I think of Milo's mouth on my mouth, but I don't want to think about Milo's mouth on my mouth so then I think of Culler's mouth on my mouth and then I feel my face going red again. "He's my best friend . . ."

"Best friend? What's wrong with him?"

"Nothing." It comes out a little stilted.

"I'm just joking."

I pick at my fries. "I'm not that great."

I hate that I said that in front of him. I hate how it sounds.

"Not hungry?" Culler asks.

"No," I say.

"Me neither." He pushes the fries away and rummages into his book bag. He pulls out a point-and-shoot digital camera—not the nice SLR he usually travels with. He turns it on and gazes at the LCD screen.

"I took the photographs out of the frames. Your dad's photographs."

He looks at me. I'm not sure if I'm supposed to give him my blessing or whatever and I try to think of a nice way to say I don't care what he does with the photos. If he burned them, I wouldn't care. The last thing my father left meant nothing to me, didn't tell me anything. And I feel like if I think about that too hard, I'll do something drastic.

"Oh."

"They were numbered on the back," Culler says. "I mean, they were ordered. It went from the barn, to the school, to the gazebo, to the empty house, to the church, to Tarver's. One, two, three, four, five, six. But we were at Tarver's first."

He hands me the point-and-shoot. It's a snapshot of the back of one of my father's photographs. There's a number on it—scribbled in his handwriting. Three. The school.

"Okay," I say.

"I decided to go to the barn, because I can't keep going to Tarver's, right? It's about twenty, thirty miles outside of Haverfield. I took some photos. It was the first time I'd been there since . . ." He leans forward. "It was almost spiritual, in a way. I can't describe it. I felt like something bigger than me was going on. Have you ever felt that way? I used to feel that about my photographs but this was even more than that—it *was* that, but it was something else . . ."

There's only one time I can remember feeling that way.

"What?" Culler asks, sensing it.

"When he died . . . I felt that . . . ," I say. Culler reaches over and squeezes my arm, but I still don't get it. "This is what was important? I don't . . ."

Culler takes the camera back from me.

"I didn't want to leave," he says. "I took photographs of every corner of that barn." He pushes a button on the camera and then hands it back to me. "And I found this."

I stare at the tiny screen.

At first, I'm not sure what I'm looking at, and then—I am.

I am looking at words, carved, etched, clawed, into a rotting piece of wood. I put the camera down and cover my mouth with my hand.

The diner feels very far away.

"Eddie," Culler says. I can't speak. He says my name again. "Eddie."

I shake my head. My eyes sting. My lower lip is trembling. I turn my face to the window, so no one else in the diner can see how fucked up I look right now. Culler gets up and sits beside me, taking the outside of the booth so no one can see me. I keep my face turned from him. I don't want him to see it any more than he has to. He leans into me.

"Okay?"

"Yes."

"It's not okay."

I turn to him. He is so close, I can see his eyelashes. His lips are close.

I hate myself for thinking that now.

"You think . . . he put that there."

"The photos are numbered," he explains, his voice quiet, careful. "They're like a map. We know he put his initials on the door in Tarver's. That was the *last* photo he numbered. The barn was first—and I find that there? I mean . . . I guess it's possible it's the weirdest, cruelest coincidence on the planet, but I don't think it is . . ."

"*Secrets on City Walls,*" I say. "That's what it reminds me of . . ."

"Yeah," Culler says. I notice his voice is shaking, like he's ready to give too—this is that hard for him. And then I feel terrible, because of course this would be that hard for him. "That's what I thought too. If the photos *are* a map, we'll have to go to each place . . . see if we can find—"

"Him?"

I wish I could take it back as soon as it's out of my mouth, but I can't. Culler freezes, deer in the headlights, and then slowly sinks back in his seat, like I've taken his essence and what's left can't keep itself upright. I don't know what to say. And then he laughs and it cuts through me because it sounds like he's about to break.

"It's fucked up that I was thinking that too," he says. "I miss him . . . so much."

"Me too," I say.

"I can't work. I can't sleep. This is—I think I'd take any answer." He takes a shuddering breath in and out. "Just any . . ."

He rests his head against my shoulder and I bring my right hand to his face, awkwardly, my palm against his cheek, my fingers at the edge of his hair. I sense people looking at us, but I don't care. I let him stay like that and I try to be the one who is together.

"I'm sorry," I say. "Culler, I'm so sorry . . ."

We stay like that for a long time and I feel his grief, the way this is all on him and I know I don't feel that with Milo, who doesn't feel this like Culler and I do.

Culler exhales slowly and raises his head. He looks like he's going to cry. We are so close, even closer than before. He leans to me for a minute, and I think he's going to kiss me but then he moves back and runs a shaking hand through his hair.

"The second photo is the school." His voice is strained. "I'm going to go there, see if I can find something. If there's nothing there—"

"Then it's nothing," I say.

But it has to be something. It *has* to be. I don't know what to call it. A note. An explanation. Art. The last thing he wanted the world to know. Me to know. His family.

My thoughts are racing, my pulse is racing.

This is what I have been waiting for.

"You have to come with me," Culler says.

We stare at each other. Everything is too much in this moment. But it's good. It's good for once. Part of me feels like I should be jumping up and down, excited, a whole world opening up, a world where the dead can speak, maybe. I look around the diner. People are eating. The world just maybe changed, and these people are acting like nothing's happened. My gaze travels over Roy Ackman at the far end of the room, shoving a burger into his face. I ran into his truck.

I want to get up and go over to him and say, *Roy, the world has changed. Maybe.*

I pick up the camera with shaking hands and stare at the LCD screen, the two words carved into that barn outside of Haverfield. I touch my fingers to them.

FIND ME
S.R.

This is the part where Beth yells at me when I step through the door.

This is the part where Mom cries on me after Beth is done yelling at me. Normal. It's so depressing how these things become normal. Like brushing your teeth. People being depressed and angry in this house is as unextraordinary as shoving a toothbrush in your mouth and running it back and forth across your teeth. It's like flossing, or getting dressed.

Mom cries on me, gaspy awful sobs against my shoulder, and her tears go straight through the material of my shirt. She says, "I went into your room to talk to you. The window was open and I didn't know where you went—I thought you were mad at me—I thought you ran away—"

All I can say is, *I'm sorry, I'm sorry, I'm so sorry,* but I don't feel it. I mean, I *am* sorry and I hate that she's crying and I hate that I worried her, but something more important has happened. I feel that more than anything else.

I go upstairs to my room and lay on the bed, fully clothed and nowhere close to sleeping even though the sooner I sleep, the sooner I wake up to go with Culler to the old, abandoned school-house that is two miles outside of Ellory and an hour outside of Haverfield to see what my father might have left for us there.

Milo calls me.

"Hi," he says, and suddenly I'm back beneath that streetlight with him and my stomach curls in on itself. He kissed me. "Beth called here, looking for you. I was so shocked to hear her voice, I fucked up and told her I didn't know where you were."

"They thought I ran away," I say. "Because I went out the window. It was bad."

"Jesus. Maybe you should start using the front door."

"Maybe."

"Were you at—" he pauses. "I mean . . . were you . . . there?"

"No."

"Where?"

I could lie to him. I should lie to him, maybe. If I don't tell him the truth and I deny I was at Tarver's, he'll just think I was at Tarver's anyway.

"Culler Evans wanted to meet me. At Chester's."

Silence.

"That student of your dad's?"

"Yeah."

"Oh," Milo says. "Chester's? Like a—I mean, why?"

This is stressing me out already. I don't even know why it's stressing me out. It shouldn't stress me out. I shouldn't care that I kissed Milo anymore. That's small and stupid and petty.

What Culler showed me, that's big. That's bigger than anything. It's so big, all I should want to do is share it with my best friend.

"Do you remember . . ." I don't even know where to start. "Do you remember when I told you that I went to Tarver's and my dad had carved his name into the door . . . ?"

He pauses. "Yeah . . ."

And then I tell him the rest, the way Culler told it to me, and it comes out of my mouth excited and urgent and hopeful, which is nothing I showed in front of Culler.

I believe in this. I do.

"What do you think?" I ask, when I'm done.

He's silent. I wish I could see his face, the shock, the way it felt. The world ending. Does it feel like that to Milo too, or is it just me? Just me and Culler.

"How did you two meet again?" he asks. "He's twenty-one?"

"That's not what I asked you."

"I don't know," he says. "I honestly have no idea."

"It's my dad, Milo." I swallow. "The place is near Ellory. The school. We're going there tomorrow to see if there's anything else—"

"I'll go with you."

The first thing I think is, *no, no, no, no, no.* And I don't know why I think that. I don't know what's wrong with me, that I wouldn't want him there.

I wanted to tell him about it, so why wouldn't I want him there?

"Eddie, he meant something to me too," Milo says.

How can I say no to that.

I call Culler. I tell him about Milo. He tells me to drive to the school with Milo and he'll meet us there and that moment in Chester's, where his head was against me and I could feel his grief, seems so far away. I feel like I've fucked up something really fundamental here, but I don't know what or how.

The house is still. After a while, I hear Beth walk past my room and into the guest room. There is a familiarity to her footsteps now and I fucking hate it, but I'm not as bothered by it as I usually am. I can't get my father's words—maybe my father's words—carved into wood out of my head. I know I'm not going to find him—I know that. He's dead. I saw him dead. I saw him that night. Dead at Tarver's. Tarver's, where he scratched his name into the door.

But if there are words between the barn and Tarver's . . . they could tell me what I need to know. They could tell me why. *Why.*

The word makes my head quiet. Every time I think it, I am met with silence. It's all I think. *Why, why, why.* Because his suicide note was nothing. It was love and giving up, but no real reason. These things don't give you peace when all is said and done. They just make you feel worse.

I get up and open my door slowly, pad down the hall and down the stairs. I open the door to my dad's office and I'm wondering about when we're going to start clearing it out and if we're ever going to clear it out, when I spot Mom sitting in his chair. Her head is against the back of it; her eyes are closed. At first I think she's dead.

And then she opens her eyes and stares at me.

"Uhm," I mumble, feeling caught. "I'll . . ."

"Did you need something?" she whispers.

I shake my head. "Did you?"

"No, I was just . . ."

"I can go."

"No, just—"

The weirdness of the situation hits us both then. I am talking to my mother like she's a stranger and I've intruded on her space and she's responding to me in the same way. Her face dissolves and she holds out her arms, but I stay where I am. I want to go to her—there are no words for how much I want to go to her—but for some reason, my feet won't move.

"What are you doing?" I ask.

"I don't know," she says. "I just miss him."

I swallow. "Me too."

"I know. I know, Eddie." She rubs her forehead and then she laughs and then she cries. "God, I don't know what I'm doing. Do I? So I don't do anything." I don't know what to say. She looks at me. "I'm not there for you. It's your father and I'm not even there for you."

"Yes, you are," I say, fidgeting, but I'm lying and she knows it.

"I know you have a hard time with Beth." She sniffles, and every second that passes is one I wish I'd never opened this door. "But she brings order. And I need that because I can't . . . I can't do that right now. You know?"

"I know."

"I know you wouldn't—you wouldn't think it, but she misses your father very much."

"I know, Mom." Robot words coming out of my robot mouth. "It's okay."

"I'll get better. This won't be . . ."

She trails off. Her eyes drift to the note on the desk, still in front of her, and a shadow passes over her face. I feel closer to my mother, in that small moment, than I ever have because I know she finds it as unsatisfying, as unacceptable as I do.

"Did I miss something?" I ask.

She looks at me. "What?"

"Was he suffering?" I feel so stupid. Of course he was suffering. You don't just choose to end your life because you're not suffering. "I mean, it's like . . ." And every time I speak her face is just more and more shattered and I don't want to continue, but I guess I have to. "I don't know who he was . . . that he'd do that."

"He was your father," she says. "He loved you. *That's* who he was."

I shake my head slowly, because that's not who he was.

And then I realize I haven't really thought of him that way in a long time. As the man who laughed and smiled and joked and valued the people he lived with. The man who did every stereotypical father cliché in the book and acted like he loved it. I don't think of him anymore. I buried him. Now it's like I'm looking for answers to a stranger's death and I couldn't tell anyone why it's so important to me, because this stranger didn't do anything for me. He never showed himself to me—this tortured artist, who hated being here so much, who could find no good in anything. He just left, killed himself, and he ruined everything. So why should I care? Why?

The disconnect is incredible and lonely.

Mom thumbs at the note.

"It's not good enough, is it."

I shake my head, but she doesn't look at me. She gets up, clutching his housecoat closed, and moves to leave.

She stops and kisses my forehead.

"I'm still here," she says.

That's another lie, though.

She leaves me alone in Dad's old office. I stand in the doorway for a long time and then I cross the room and sit in his chair. It's still warm, from her sitting in it. I try to feel the place as it would feel if he were still alive. I pick up the note.

He had to go. He loves us forever. Who writes that? I don't know who this person is, but I know my father is underneath it somewhere, and I miss him.

I have to get him back.

I close my eyes and think of the photograph Culler showed me. I see it in my head perfectly. He'll be there, at that school. Another piece of my father. And then another. Six pieces. I will find them all, put them together. I'll find him.

And then I'll let him go.

The first half of the trip to Ellory is uncomfortable because there isn't enough space between me and Milo. At the same time, there's too much of it, an ocean of it, and that feels as alien as being close. I think I kind of hate him for it. The kiss between us has totally fucked me up; I am too aware of my body around him. Every time I move, it's awkward. I think of him touching me. And the most annoying thing about it is I know it's totally one-sided. He is totally relaxed beside me, like these thoughts aren't all in his head, and it's not fair. It's giving me a stomachache.

"Are you nervous about this?" Milo asks after a while.

"I'm ready."

He pauses. "What if it's not what you want it to be?"

"It's already what I want it to be," I say. "It's . . . more."

"So did you tell your mom and Beth you'd be out all day, or did you climb out through the window again?"

"I told them I was with you," I say. It's all I told them. *I'm spending the day with Milo. Bye.* And then I left before anyone could say anything, and I met him at Fuller's. I roll down the window and let warm air fill the car.

"I Googled Culler Evans," Milo says.

"Really?" He would.

"The artist's statement was fucking pretentious. Art at all costs? You have to be brave enough to look at his art? What does that even mean?"

"Actually, my dad loved that statement," I say. "It's why he took Culler on."

That shames him. A little. "Maybe I don't get it. His photos weren't that great."

"That is a really subjective thing," I say. It comes out of my mouth maybe a little more defensive than I want it to. "I mean, you can't say that definitively. It's . . . art."

"Well, what did you think of his *art*?"

"I think he's talented. Do you think they were staged? The photos?"

"I hope so. Some of them were kind of fucked up . . ." He pauses. "Some of them were fucked up even if they were posed, though. Who takes photos of people fucking?"

"I have no idea," I deadpan. "Culler Evans surely must be the first person to do *that*."

"Oh, fuck off," he says, smiling.

I roll up the window and lean my head against the glass, tapping my fingers on my knee. I chew my lip. My stomachache has evolved. Milo has no part of it anymore—it's just about my dad now. I don't feel well. I thought I'd be excited, but I'm not.

This is all taking too long.

I want to get this over with.

"It'll be okay," Milo says. He knows what I'm thinking and he reaches over, touches my arm reassuringly, and I shiver and when I look at him, he's not looking at me.

"Thanks," I mutter.

It takes us forever to find the school. I tell Culler we'll be there at two, but it's already three by the time we arrive, and I cringe because he mentioned something about not wanting to lose the light. When we get to the school, Culler is standing in front of it. His back is to us, his arms are up. I know what he's doing.

"He's taking *pictures*?" Milo asks, pulling up next to Culler's station wagon, which is parked on the grass next to the building. Almost as if he can hear Milo, Culler turns and waves. His trusty Nikon is around his neck. My heart thuds.

I get out of the car without a word to Milo.

"Did you find it?" I ask. Culler takes my picture, but I don't care.

"I wasn't going to look without you," he says. "Wouldn't feel right."

Milo gets out of the car. "So this is the place?"

"Yeah," Culler says. "I was here . . . the last time he was here."

He makes his way to Milo and extends his hand. They shake. Milo is tense, completely stiff. Culler notices and gives Milo a friendly smile. I think.

"It's good to meet you, Milo," he says. "Eddie talks about you a lot."

"Yeah." Milo glances at me and I want to die because I don't know how he's taking that, and also, it's a lie, and then Milo lies to Culler: "Likewise . . ."

Awkward. The three of us stare at the school. It's nothing special. It's all run-down. White siding, but the paint has been flaking for who knows how long and all the wood beneath it is rotting. The roof is metal and starting to rust. I imagine it when it was new, a nice place. On rainy days it must've sounded unreal, loud. Like the world was ending.

Four windows line the left side of the school and, I'm sure, the right of it. The windows are broken or boarded up or missing altogether. The entrance is foreboding. The left door has been boarded up. The right door has been ripped off its hinges and rests next to the building, like it's waiting for someone to put it back on.

I see hints of the ruin inside.

And then I'm completely overcome with the fact that my father stood here, left something of himself here. Was he ready to go when he came here? I think I understand what Culler meant when he said it was almost spiritual, except I don't feel spiritual so much as I feel like his death is on me. So much I think I'm going to die. I don't want to die.

I don't want to die.

The thought steals my breath away, and I'm gulping air and that thought gets louder and louder. *I don't want to die.* And a worse thought: *will it hurt?* Like he's inside my head. Did he ask these questions? What if it hurt? What if—

"Eddie?" Milo moves to me. "Eddie—"

And then I am half-choking on air, half-trying not to. And then Culler is there and I try to tell him it's okay, I'm okay, but the words seem to escape me and he has his arm on my shoulder, trying to force my head between my knees while telling me to do the same.

"Put your head between your knees—just—between your knees—" But I keep trying to straighten, because this is embarrassing. But I can't breathe. "Eddie, calm down and just do what I tell you. Breathe in—okay, good—breathe out—"

I do as he tells me. Breathe in. Okay. Good. Breathe out. Eventually, I feel the ground beneath my feet and all the mortification that comes with the clarity after a moment like this. Milo is completely concerned, which makes me anxious, but when I look at Culler, he looks like he understands—like it's not a big deal—which makes me feel calmer. A little.

"I'm sorry." My voice is weak and shaky. "I'm sorry—"

"Why?" Milo asks. "You have nothing to be sorry about."

I take a deep breath, stumble on nothing. Milo grabs my arm and steadies me.

"Sit down," Culler orders. "You need a minute. I'll . . . take more photos."

I nod feebly and sink down to the grass, facing the entrance to the school. Milo sits next to me. Culler squeezes my shoulder and gives us space.

"Are you okay?" Milo asks.

"I'm fine."

"Bullshit."

"I know, it's just—" I rub my forehead. "I really felt it."

"Felt what?"

"Everything." It sounds like I'm going to cry, but I'm not. But I hate that it sounds like that. "Sometimes it's too much."

"I know."

"No, you don't."

He's quiet for a minute. "Eddie, give me some credit."

The way he says it kills me and I don't know what to say to that—or if I even can say anything to that. I just got myself back. I don't want to sad-fight with him.

"Should you be doing this?" he asks.

"Milo, don't—"

"I know you're going to do it no matter what, but do you think you *should* be doing this?"

He brushes a strand of hair from my face, and I move from his touch. His face turns pink and I feel even worse because neither of us can pretend that didn't happen. I didn't do it because it was him, though. Because I'm still awkward about our kiss. I did it because I don't want to be touched. He'd never believe me if I told him that, though. But it's true.

I think.

"You totally look wrecked and we haven't even found anything yet," he says.

"I'm *fine*."

"And I was serious, when we were in the car," Milo says. "What if what you find isn't what you want it to be?"

"Why are you asking me this stuff?" I get to my feet, prickling. "Can you give it a chance before you write it off? It's important to me."

"Eddie, I didn't—" His eyes travel past me, to something else, and then he says, "I don't want my fucking photograph taken, thanks."

I turn. Culler is nearby, camera aimed at us. He looks a little caught.

"No disrespect meant." He lowers his camera. "It's just how I process. I won't do it again."

He faces the school and takes another shot of it.

"That's fucking creepy," Milo says, not even bothering to lower his voice. Culler isn't close enough to overhear, but still.

"It's not a big deal," I say. "You heard him, it's just how he processes . . ."

Milo gives me this look. This *You like him* look, but he doesn't say it. But I think he's close to saying it, and I so cannot hear him say that. I clear my throat.

"I think we should go in," I say loudly. "We should go in and see what we find."

Culler makes his way over to us.

"We'll find him," he says.

He is so—I don't know. Perfect. Everything about him is perfect. The shape of his mouth, which has kissed me. His hair, which looks unruly and unbrushed but on purpose. And then I remember all the dirty pavement sex I imagined us having after he kissed me and *what is wrong with me*? I feel completely bipolar.

I step through the open door and into the schoolhouse—a one-room schoolhouse. Old. Light floods in through the open windows. Dust motes float in those rays of sunlight. It's hard to take in so much decay; I'm not sure where to start. The walls are browning or water-stained or something and the plaster curls in on itself. In some places, there are holes in the wall.

You can see the wall beneath the wall.

There's a scratched-up blackboard at the front of the room. It's been spray-painted. Not my father's handiwork, I don't think, but it fits him somehow . . . someone spray-painted a stick figure staring up at birds overhead. It's so disaffected looking, like a teenager tried really hard to make it look like a kid did it. The word DREAMS is on one side of the stick figure and someone else spray-painted

the words FUCKING FAGGOT with an arrow pointing to the stick figure on the other side of it, which depresses me.

On the floor beneath the old blackboard are planks of wood,
another door off its hinges, and old wooden crates. Garbage is
scattered everywhere, but there's a suspiciously tidy-looking corner. I imagine people coming here to drink and smoke. It just
seems like they would.

There are no desks, though. At the back of the room, there are
rusty hooks for coats and beneath that, a pile of old books and a
cheap-looking skateboard with no wheels.

"This is exactly how it was when I was here with him," Culler
says. "Not one thing has changed. Crazy . . ."

"Where do you think we should look?" I ask.

Culler shrugs and takes a photograph of the place.

"I don't know."

"Where did you find the one in the barn?" Milo asks him.

"It wasn't in plain sight," Culler says. "It was on the corner of
one of the doors."

We turn to the boarded-up side of the door. Milo gets there
first, his eyes traveling over every inch of space. Culler turns to me
and says, "We should each take a side. It'll be faster."

I nod and then I start combing through the left side of the
room, running my hand over the jagged wooden windowsills and
the chipping plaster. Milo stays at the boarded-up door and Culler
takes the right side of the room. We search in silence for what feels
like a long time and no one finds anything. I can't stand the thought
of ending up empty-handed. I have to leave this place with something. If I don't, I'll die.

And then Milo sneezes and startles the fuck out of us.

"Sorry." He sounds stuffed up. "I don't think there's anything
over here."

"Are you sure?" I ask.

"Yes." He sounds irritated.

Silence again. After a while, Culler makes his way over to me, smiling at me a little, and my stomach twinges. I wonder if he found something but then I think he wouldn't be smiling at me if he did.

"You scared me back there," he tells me. "I was trying to keep cool."

"You were cool," I say. "I'm sorry about Milo. He doesn't . . . he doesn't get it, you know?" I force a laugh. "Like, your portfolio went right over his head."

"You checked out my portfolio?" Culler asks.

"Yeah. It was really intense. Uncomfortable."

"That's great."

"Really?"

"Yeah, otherwise what's the point?" He looks at his camera. "That makes my day, actually. I don't want you to look at them and feel nothing."

Were they all posed? I swallow the question. I don't know why. Somehow, it seems too personal to ask that. To ask him to reveal what's behind his photographs. Like, you don't just ask a photographer to demystify his work. You either buy in or you don't.

"Some people don't get it, though," Culler adds, nodding at Milo. "It's okay. I didn't mean to make him uncomfortable. Some people really hate the camera. It's fair."

"It's how you process," I echo.

"It's about all I've got to process with lately, since I'm so blocked on my work. Everything makes more sense to me when it's a photograph," Culler admits, and he actually shifts a little, awkward and open, and I want to hug him. "I hate telling people that because they think it's a crutch that means I can't deal, but things are honestly clearer to me. I can't fathom being here, doing this, without my Nikon whether or not these pictures turn into art . . ."

"I get it," I say. I think I do.

Culler leans forward and brings his mouth close to my ear.

"You get me."

My legs feel weak. I want to melt.

"I'm not finding anything," Milo calls.

"*He* actually makes a lot of sense through the lens," Culler says, moving back. He smiles. "I think he likes you. He looks at you that way."

And then my face turns about a thousand shades of red. I clear my throat and point to the camera, desperate to change the subject.

"So you're not working on anything right now? You're still stuck?"

"Yeah. It's like I said, it doesn't seem important. *This* is what is important." He gestures around the room and my heart aches for him because I know how much it sucks to have this thing consume every part of you. This question. To have it keep you from the thing you really love to do just makes it that much worse and I'm glad I don't create. I'm just glad. He squeezes my arm. "It's okay, Eddie. We'll figure this out and it'll be okay, I promise." I think, *God, I hope so.* "Anyway, we should keep looking."

He moves past me to examine the far wall, the windowsills. I do a slow crawl around the room, worried I'm looking too hard or not hard enough. I'm worried that something is here and I'll miss it. I'm worried nothing is here. I feel the slow passage of time as we look for a ghost, my father's ghost. I think another hour must go by in total, focused silence.

I've made my way to the blackboard, when something catches my eye on the wall beside it. Small little markings that, as I get closer, reveal themselves to be words.

"Oh," I say.

Milo and Culler are next to me in a second.

We stare at what I've found.

ALL OF THESE THINGS
GONE COLD AND NOW I'M
S.R.

Culler takes a photograph. To process it.

I think Milo is in it, but he doesn't protest. He's totally shocked. His silence speaks such volumes. He thought this was a nothing trip, I know it. He didn't believe in this and I'll ask him about that later. I run my fingers over the letters again and again and again, hands shaking, until Culler finally suggests we go outside. I want to ask him if this is what it felt like for him, finding the first message. My heart is pumping pure adrenaline and I want to scream, but I can't because no sound I make could be big enough for what I'm feeling.

We sit on the grass and stare at the school.

"What does that even mean?" Milo asks after a minute.

"I don't know," Culler says.

"What's the next place?" I ask Culler. "We should go there. Like now."

"The gazebo."

"You know where that is?"

"Yeah. I figured it out. It's six hours from here," Culler says. "It would be a trip."

"But when can we go?"

"Eddie," Milo says, and I stare at him. He stares back at me and then he runs his hands through his hair. "It's just—S.R. could be anyone . . ."

"I don't think so," Culler says. "He did the same thing for—"

"Secrets on City Walls," I finish. "It can't be a coincidence."

Head rush. I feel every word of saying that so much, I have to close my eyes. Milo touches my shoulder and I force myself to open them and he moves his hand.

"I mean, it's him," I say.

"Yeah." Culler digs into his pocket and pulls out a tiny notepad and a pen. He scribbles down what we've found, even though he took a photograph. This feels weirdly absurd—like in the movies, this would be a high-stakes drama mystery. Letters from a dead man and the three of us playing detectives, seeking it out. Real life is always quieter and anticlimactic somehow.

But devastating all the same.

Culler hands me the notepad—he's written both messages so we can get a look at them connected—and it slips through my fingers. Dead hands. I wonder if this is forever. I'll go through life with my hands like this because it's not something you can just cure, I don't think. Only live with.

"Maybe you should see a doctor about that," Culler says, picking up the notebook. I rub my hands together. "Are they numb or what?"

"She doesn't need to see a doctor," Milo says.

"And you'd know that, because you're one yourself."

"No," I say, and they both look at me. "I mean—Milo's right."

"Then why are they fucked up?"

"I can't tell you. Milo doesn't like that story and I only know half of it."

"Eddie, come on," Milo says.

"Tell me the half you know," Culler says.

"It's none of your business," Milo snaps.

Culler whistles. "Testy. Are you always this testy?"

"It's from when I found my dad," I blurt out, before Milo can say anything back. My hands come back to me then. I take the notebook from Culler and stare hard at the words, like they'd tell me more than what's on there.

FIND ME / ALL THESE THINGS GONE COLD AND NOW I'M / S.R.

That doesn't even make any sense. But it will.

It *will*.

I mean, it has to.

"You found your dad?" Culler asks. I jolt back to this conversation. Milo is glaring at me, but Culler looks really intrigued. "What was that like?"

"Seriously," Milo says. "Eddie, what are you—"

"I found my dad," I say, "and Milo found me."

"Really?"

"Yeah, it was . . ." I shrug and the way Culler is looking at me is like he needs to know and that makes me want to tell him. "I mean, I wasn't there when it happened."

"How soon after?"

"I don't . . ." I honestly don't know. "I think he was cold."

"You think?"

"Eddie," Milo says again.

"I think he was cold," I say. "But his hands felt warm to me. But I think he must've actually been cold. I don't know . . ."

Culler leans forward. "I don't understand."

I laugh. I don't know why I laugh. It's a shock of sound coming out of my mouth and I feel truly self-conscious, like I'm about to turn myself inside out. I can't stand the way Milo is looking at me. I'm not looking at him, but I know how he's looking at me.

"I found him and I . . ." I rip out tufts of grass with my hand.

Plain speaking is the worst. This is the first time I've really said it out loud. ". . . lay next to him and I held his hands."

Culler stares at me in amazement.

"I don't know why," I add hastily, because it sounds sort of . . . wrong. Weird. Maybe it was, but I can't change that it was the first thing my head told my body to do before it all shut down. "It's just—what I did, and now my hands are fucked up. I'm not stupid, I know it's totally in my head, but . . ." I shake my head. "Everything after that is sort of tangled up. Like, pieces. I don't really remember. Milo knows it but . . ."

He won't tell me.

Culler turns to Milo and I know what's coming next. "What's the other half of the story? That you won't tell her?"

"It's none of your business," Milo says for the hundredth time.

Culler nods at me. "Maybe so, but isn't it hers?"

I don't say anything, as much as I agree. It's mine. It's mine because it happened to me, but Milo won't tell me. I stare at him and Milo realizes I'm not going to help him out of this. Or pretend it's okay. It's not okay that he won't tell me.

It's mine.

"Okay, fine: you were in shock," Milo says, and it's like gutting me. He just puts it all out there like that, when I know it was more than just that. "I called 911. That's it."

I get up and walk away from them and keep walking because I need to be away from Milo right now. I'm sick and shaky, angry. It's the scary kind of calm anger that almost always ends up badly if you stick around. They give me space, for a moment. I get to the other side of the school when Milo shows up and says, "Are we going now?"

"'You were in shock,'" I say. It comes out as weak when I was hoping it would come out a cuttingly accurate imitation of him. "'I called 911. That's it.' That's it? That's so it, you can just say it now but you've been blowing me off about it since it—"

"Look, I'm sorry," Milo says. "But you made me do it and I'm not sharing my life with that douchebag and *you're* not sharing my life with him, okay?"

"You don't even know him!"

"And how long have *you* known him? Since second grade?"

"Jealous?"

That is so pathetic, but it's all I have.

"Eddie, *stop* it," he snaps. "I'm not doing this here."

"Why not? This is the best place to do it."

"And that's another thing," Milo says, because I guess he just can't help himself. "This doesn't seem at all fucked up to you?"

"No. It seems perfectly normal to me."

"It's fucked up," he repeats.

"Why are you even here then?" I ask. "If all this stuff about my dad bothers you this much?"

"Eddie, I'm not here for your dad."

"I thought he meant something to you."

"What else was I going to say? Okay, fine, Eddie, you go off with this—how old is he again? This twenty-something pretentious art fuck who looks at you like—" He stops. "No—you're right, it's about your dad. You're right. I'm sorry."

"So . . ." I pause. "It's only about my dad when it's not about you."

It's so quiet between us.

"He did mean something to me. I liked your dad," Milo says. "I loved your dad. He was great. He treated me like a member of your family. I was never an imposition. And when my dad moved out, he took me aside one day and told me if I needed anything just to ask. I miss him too. A lot."

I try to remember this man Milo is talking about. For a second, something inside of me—I remember my dad, taking a moment to smile at both me and my mom before going off to do whatever he did. He'd just pause and appreciate . . .

And then Milo ruins it: "But if he left messages for you to torture yourself with . . . I think less of him."

I can't believe he just said that.

"Then maybe you should go back to Branford," I say.

"I'm not leaving without you."

"Well, I'm not going with you. So."

He laughs bitterly. "Wow. You like him, don't you?"

"I—"

"You like him," he repeats.

He's hurt. I look away.

"Milo—"

"It's fine," he says, shrugging. "I'm just saying."

"Well, what do you want me to say? You still make me feel alone," I say. "And you're not honest with me—"

"I'm not honest with you?" Milo asks, but the way he asks it is the worst. Like it's a question that doesn't mean anything, and the answer only vaguely interests him.

"You keep things from me. You won't tell me about that night . . ."

"Did you ever—" He makes a frustrated noise and buries his face in his hands, and when he lowers his hands, he is so sad. I hate seeing that on him. "Did you ever think that maybe it's hard for me?" he asks. "Eddie, I can't stand to think of you the way I found you that night. I think half the time you forget it happened to *me* too."

And that makes me cry. I brush the tears away, frantic, and he reaches for me and I move back from him and I look at him, but I can't stand to look at him. I can't do this with him. It's too hard.

"Don't—you're right. I'm sorry. But you should go back," I say, walking away from him. "I don't want you here . . ."

"Eddie—"

"No, go *back*, Milo. I can't—I'll be fine."

I walk around the school and lean against it, covering my face with my hands, crying stupid, until I hear Milo's car start up and leave. I wipe at my eyes and try to calm down enough to find Culler, but when I look up, he's there, his camera resting against his chest.

"That sounded intense," he says.

"You were listening?"

"I didn't catch all the words," he says. "But it sounded intense. And now he's gone, so I don't think I'm wrong . . . ?"

"I don't want to talk about it."

"That's fine."

"I don't have a ride home."

"Yes, you do."

Culler reaches forward and runs his thumbs over the top of my hands, like they don't belong to me, and I feel different parts of my heart separating into pieces, like the piece that's with Milo in his car, the piece that knows why I stayed here and let him go, the piece that likes Culler touching me, and the piece that remembers the last and first time he kissed me. So many pieces.

I let him take a photograph of my hands.

I don't know why.

Culler asks me back to his apartment. My thoughts are so far from home and this is maybe the strangest day of my life, so I say, *yes, of course.*

"I have two roommates," Culler says. "Stella is cool—she's a musician. But Topher is kind of . . ." He trails off. "He's a photographer. He thinks he's better than me because he goes to school for it." I don't really get it and Culler smiles a little. "You know how they say don't bring up politics and religion at the dinner table?" I nod. "Well, those are the topics people change the subject *to* when Topher and I get into it about photography."

"I'm really glad I'm not an artist," I say.

"No, you're a work of art."

If anyone else said that to me, I think I'd roll my eyes, but Culler saying it to me means me committing it to memory and locking it inside so I'll always have it.

It takes a while to get back to Haverfield. By the time we do, the city he lives in is cast in a late-afternoon glow. His apartment building is a surprisingly nice place. For some reason, I pictured something a lot more starving artist, but I guess he must do okay.

"Rent paid for by my parents," Culler says. Or that. "Think less of me?"

"I don't think less of you."

His apartment is on the third floor. I'm really nervous all of a sudden, realizing quickly how this is going to look. Unless Culler brings seventeen-year-old girls up to his apartment all the time. And now I am going to bleach that thought out of my head.

"It's me," Culler calls as he opens the door. I follow him inside. He takes off his shoes at the door, so I do too. "I brought someone. Hope that's okay with you guys."

"Do they bite?" A girl asks. Stella.

"No. It's not okay with me." That must be Topher. "Send them out."

I take in Culler's place. It's small and minimalist. Photographs line the cream walls. I don't think they're Culler's photos, though. They seem too innocuous. The kitchen and living room are separated by a beaded curtain and I make out the shapes of two people on a couch. Culler takes me by the hand and pulls me through the beads, which brush against my arms, my face. I like his hand around my hand.

Stella and Topher look around Culler's age. Stella might be older. Her long black hair has been gathered up in a side bun. She's wearing this really nice summer dress. Topher is exactly how I imagined him, based on Culler's brief description of his attitude alone. An *artiste*. He's dressed all in black and he has short, curly brown hair and his mouth looks kind of sneery.

"Jailbait?" The first thing he says to me. It shocks me into silence.

"No, her name is Eddie Reeves," Culler replies, rolling his eyes. "Eddie, this is Stella Teng and Topher Green."

"Do you bite?" Stella asks me.

"No," I say.

She smiles. "Good to know."

"Wait a second," Topher says slowly. "Reeves . . . as in . . . ?"

"I'm his daughter," I say. "I mean, if that's who you're talking about . . ."

"Oh," Stella says softly. "I'm sorry for your loss."

"Thank you."

Topher doesn't say anything, but he keeps staring at me in a way that makes me feel really uncomfortable. Culler touches my back and says, "Drink?"

"Yes, please."

He disappears back into the kitchen. I shift.

"Culler says you're a musician," I say to Stella. "I think that's really cool."

"Thank you, so much," she says.

"What does he say about me?" Topher asks. I open my mouth and then I close it because I'm trying to make a decent impression. Topher snorts. "I thought so."

Culler comes back with a pitcher of bright green liquid and glasses and pours a drink for each of us. I sip mine. Vodka and Gatorade. Tastes like high school.

"Like, how old are you?" Topher asks, watching me drink. "Fifteen?"

"Fuck off, Topher," Culler says.

"Boys, boys." Stella pats the space next to her. I smile gratefully and sit down. "Culler showed me some of your father's work. It was really amazing how he took over a whole city, just to get it all out there."

"Are you a photographer?" Topher asks me.

"No. Not really. At all." I laugh nervously. Culler is glaring at Topher. This is really strange. "I don't really get art. I don't know."

"That's weird," Topher says. "Did that bother your father?"

"No. Why would it?"

He shrugs. "I don't know. Following in his footsteps and everything . . ."

"Is your father pissed you're not an accountant?" Culler asks. Topher flips Culler off. I can't even tell if they're friends or not.

Culler turns to me. "Topher's extremely jealous, because where he gets to be taught *about* the Late Seth Reeves, I got to be taught *by* him."

"You were taught about my dad?" I ask Topher.

"We briefly analyzed his later work and then his name came up once after he died," Topher says. "That's all."

"Really?"

"Mostly speculation about why he killed himself."

"Any interesting theories?" I have to know.

"Eddie," Culler says. "Nothing Topher says is interesting."

"You really want to know?"

I finish off the drink before I nod. Yes. I want to know. It's all I want to know.

"Uninspired, tortured artist. Walking cliché." Topher doesn't even try to soften the blow, not even a little. "His grand pronouncement about leaving the art scene behind so he could 'give his art back to himself' was an excuse. He was dried up artistically."

"Oh," I whisper. Stella tops off my drink.

"But then, how bad off do you have to be if you think Culler's work has any kind of merit whatsoever—"

"Hey," Culler says sharply. "I know you're taking the piss, man, but Eddie might not and that's her father you're talking about, okay?"

Topher manages a look of contrition. "Sorry."

"I needed to know," I mumble.

But I don't think I can forgive him for what he said. Culler grabs my hand and pulls me to my feet. "Come on, I'll show you my room."

Part of me really hopes that's a line.

Culler takes me to his room. There are no clothes all over the floor—not that kind of mess—but there are books everywhere. A futon against the wall. He has two desks. One with a computer and two monitors. The other desk is full of his equipment. A little tripod rests on its side. Some lenses and digital camera bodies just sitting out. I swear one of them looks like it's collecting dust. Tiny memory cards—digital film. Some photographs have been printed, here and there. It's so unorganized; almost careless.

"I know," Culler says because he knows what I'm thinking. He always knows what I'm thinking. How is that? "I need to be better about that."

Next to the wall beside his equipment are the photographs I gave him. The photographs my father took. Tarver's looks out at me. The schoolhouse—I see it through my dad's eyes and it's nothing like what I saw today. The place looks silvery, the way he used the light. Silvery gray and so sharp, like it's more clear about anything than I will ever be.

I open my mouth to say that, but instead I say, "I like your photographs better."

"Oh—uhm, wow," Culler says, surprised. "I mean—thank you. So much."

"I like the photo of the couple. Together." I don't know where I get off saying that, but I do. I feel a little heady from the drink-and-a-half, brave. "Who were they?"

Culler smiles faintly. "Well—one of them was me . . ."

I'm speechless for a second. The two vague, unidentifiable people having sex—one of them was Culler. I have this funny thought: I wish the girl were me. I have this other thought: oh my God, that was real. I have a thought on top of that: if that was real, what about the other photos? The one in the hospital, the woman attacked . . .

Culler clears his throat.

"Anyway. We've done Tarver's and we've done the school, and the gazebo"—he points to it—"is about six hours away from here, in a place called Valleyview. About three hours south of Valleyview is the house. That's in Labelle. The church is in Lissie, and Lissie is about four hours from Labelle."

"How did you figure this out?" I ask.

"I was with him for some of them. Those were easy. The gazebo was hard, but the water tower—see it way back there? First three letters on it, VALL—gave it away . . ."

"You're like a Hardy Boy," I say. He smiles. "When do we go?"

"It's a lot of driving. I think we need a plan of action . . ."

A phone rings from another room. Nobody gets it.

"Probably my dad," Culler tells me. "I'll be right back."

He slips out and leaves me alone with the photographs. The room feels small now. Just me, and the last art my father created, if you can even call it art. I crouch down and press my fingers to the face of each photograph, like I could go to these places just by touch. I want to stretch this whole thing out forever, but I want it to be over. I don't know. All I know is I don't want to be in this room alone much longer with these photos. I leave and meet Topher, who is coming out of what I guess is his room at the same time.

"So how old are you, seriously?" He asks. "Fifteen?"

"I'm seventeen," I mutter.

"You really think he's talented?"

"Culler?" I ask. Topher nods. "I think he's amazing." Topher smiles, like that's amusing to him, and I blurt out, "Do you hate Culler or something?"

"I don't hate Culler, no." He pauses. "Think of us as friendly rivals. We both applied to the same schools. Ask him to show you all his rejections." He shrugs. "He thinks I'm wasting my money. I think anyone can put a photo up on a Web site."

"Art should be shared." I raise my chin. "My father believed that."

"Speaking of your father, that's why I'm here. I forgot to tell you something—we thought he was *scared* too," Topher says. "That's why he killed himself. And I wouldn't have bothered to tell you, but you said you needed to know."

And then he walks down the hall and I'm still.

Scared.

My father wasn't scared.

Was he?

No. But—

What if he *was* scared, all the time. For years, until he couldn't take it anymore. What was he scared of? What could scare him so bad about living that he'd do that? What if he wasn't tired, but just full of fear no one could talk him out of.

I can't stand to think of him scared.

So I think of that gazebo, the next place. Valleyview. My cell rings. I step back into Culler's room and I turn to the window. The sky is turning a deeper blue. Early evening. I just stare at it for a minute before answering. It's not Milo. It's Beth.

"Where *are* you?" she hisses.

"How did you get my number?"

"That doesn't matter. Where are you?"

"Why?"

"Milo called and told me you've run off with some strange boy in Haverfield—"

"*What?*"

"That's what I'd like to know! What are you *doing?*—"

"Okay, Beth," I say, glancing at the door. "First of all, I'm not with some strange boy. I'm with—" *Lie.* I don't know why. That's what my brain is telling me to do—if not lie, don't tell the whole truth. "I'm with a friend—"

"What?"

"I'm with friends."

"A friend or friends? Who?"

"It doesn't matter. Everything is fine."

"Oh." For once I've got Beth completely out of her element. She can only talk to me from there. She can't stop me from doing anything or tell me what to do. She can't make me come back. Even better: at any point, I could hang up on her. "But I—"

"Everything is fine."

"The way Milo put it—"

"Milo was wrong. It's fine."

I'm not mad at Milo about this. Not right now, anyway. Maybe later. Probably later, when I'm closer. It's like, this far away from him, I can't even be mad.

I like this distance.

"Oh." I can hear Beth breathing on the other end of the line. "Because your mother can't take any messing around, Eddie. Not after the stunt you pulled the other night. Do you know what that did to her? Do you know what it would do to her *again*—"

"Beth," I say impatiently, "I'm not—"

"I mean, what is this, Eddie? You just go to Haverfield on a whim, have fun with a few friends, leave Milo to go back on his—"

"Beth, I'm hanging up—"

"No—don't you *dare*. I'm not finished yet—"

I stay on the line, white hot fury in my gut.

"Then finish."

"When will you be coming back?"

"I'm not." I don't even think it. Just say it.

"What?!"

I have to hold the phone away from my ear. The idea has me before I have it. It gets tangled up in my stomach. It feels impossibly urgent. I try to swallow, and I can't.

I'm not coming back.

I don't have to come back.

"I'm not coming back."

"You just said—"

"I changed my mind," I say. "I'm not—"

"Your mother—"

"I don't care. I'm not coming back."

"Eddie, I will call the police—"

"Can she handle that? Mom? If you did that?" This must be that attitude Beth was talking about, but I don't care. "Would she get out of her housecoat ever again, you think?"

"Have you lost your *mind*? This isn't funny—"

"I'm staying in Haverfield for a few days and you're going to cover for me—"

"Eddie—"

"Or I won't come home at all."

I hang up before she can say anything else. My heart pounds in my chest and when I turn around, Culler is behind me. I feel awake, I feel so awake and alive, like I can breathe after ages of not being able to breathe, and I wonder if this is how Milo felt when he ran away from home in the third grade, like if whatever was suffocating him there just magically stopped as soon as he made that choice—to just go.

But this isn't running away. Not yet.

But it could be.

"I can take you back," Culler says, and I don't know how much he's heard. "Whenever you want to go."

"How about a few days from now?"

He laughs. "As tempting as that is—"

"I'm serious."

He waits for me to continue. I feel nervous, sick. But he'll say yes to this. I know he will. He has to. He started this. He brought it to me, so he has to.

"Because I told them I wasn't coming home—"

His smile vanishes. "Eddie—"

"They're covering for me." I bite my lip. That's a lie, maybe. I don't know yet if Beth will cover for me. But I think she will, because she knows I'm right. My mom is too fragile for this. She'd break. We'd never be able to put her back together. But if I find what I'm looking for, that's a risk I'm willing to take. "For a few days, until—"

"I could put you up . . ."

"No—"

"I'm not going to let you wander around Haverfield without anywhere to stay—"

"It's so we can finish," I interrupt. Part of me feels really warm at the thought that he wouldn't just let me fumble, that if I only told him I needed to be away from home, he'd let me be away from home here, with him. "We could do Valleyview, Labelle, and Lissie.

Get to those places and see what he left behind. Just get in the car. Go."

"A road trip," he says. "That's what you mean."

"I have money," I say really fast. "I'd pay for everything. Gas, food, motel—whatever. Just—I can't wait all summer. And when I go back home, I'll probably be in trouble, so I don't have a lot of time. You'd have to drive and I can't and—" I swallow. "You have to be there . . . I mean, you have to." I grab his arm, like I could convince him to do this just by touching him. "Culler, it needs to be you."

He stares at me a long time and for a second, I worry he thinks I've lost my mind.

But then he asks, "When should we leave?"

Minutes after I tell him we should go. That's when we decide to leave.

It's simple. It's not.

Culler packs a bag of things and we realize I need things and a bag to pack them in. I spend an hour on the main street, going into the last of the open stores, buying, buying, buying up, while he gets ready at the apartment. I get an overnight bag and clothes—nothing fancy—toothbrush, deodorant, hairbrush. I think I spend too much, but I need it all and besides, I got something—money—when my dad died. I just never thought I'd be able to spend it.

This way feels okay because it's for him.

For as quickly as we prepare, it all takes too much time. Culler thinks I'm covered—I told him I was—but I feel Beth hovering. I feel like I'm waiting for her to change her mind. And then I get the text from Milo, and he throws a wrench into all my plans.

I'M COMING TO GET YOU.

I text him back.

ALREADY GONE. IT'S OK. I PROMISE.

I wait.

CAN I CALL?
TALK WHEN I'M BACK.
BETH ASKED ME TO COVER FOR YOU. SHE'S GIVING YOU
A WEEK.

I feel a rush of relief. THANK YOU.
And then: I'M GIVING YOU TWO DAYS.

"We have to go," I tell Culler. "Milo is going to ruin everything."
"Unsurprising development," he comments.
"It's surprising to me," I mumble.
Culler thinks of all these things I don't. He packs a cooler full of water and food and sunscreen, so we don't bake in the car in the day, which I never would have thought of. He packs his camera and tells me it's the minimum, but a lot of things seem to go with it—extra lenses, lens covers, memory cards, chargers. Just everything. I watch him put it all in the backseat. All this to help him process. I envy him that. I wish I had something to process this through. He even packs the photos my father took. Just in case, he tells me.
And then everything is in the car except us.
We stand outside the station wagon, neither of us moving. This is a big moment and I don't think we know how to say it. There are sounds all around us. Haverfield is a different place at night than Branford. People talk and walk the street, laughing. Enjoying the summer.
"Okay," Culler says.
That's it.
We get in the car.
It feels like being in one of the funeral cars, with my mom.

Parked behind the hearse, waiting to pull out in traffic. Holding her hand. It's not exactly like that, but it feels like that. One of those moments where you know things are going to be so different afterward. When I found my dad, I knew things were going to change forever, but sitting next to her, getting ready to see him buried, I felt it in a different way. Everything ached.

This reminds me of that—how it aches.

But it's a better ache, too.

I'm hopeful.

I can't remember the last time I felt hopeful.

The ride to Valleyview is quiet. Maybe because it's night and because there are so few cars on the road. Maybe Culler needs to absorb this in silence because it's happening to him too.

Six hours of road are stretched ahead of us and it's starting to sink in, what I've done. Milo texts me as soon as we pass the THANK YOU FOR VISITING HAVERFIELD! sign. It's like he can sense that I've reached that point of no return. We go back and forth.

PLEASE LET ME CALL.
NOT A GOOD TIME.
WHY?
ON THE ROAD.
WHERE?
DOESN'T MATTER. EVERYTHING'S OK.

My stomach twists with guilt. Beth probably made it sound bad, what I said to her. But he knows me. He should know I only kind of meant it.

Streetlights disappear. The farther we get from Haverfield, the more stars there are. I roll down the window and rest my head against the frame, hoping the mild summer air will keep me awake. I'm crashing, but it wouldn't be fair to Culler to fall asleep.

"So," Culler says after a while, and I turn my face from the window. "When we get to Valleyview we'll find a motel and look for the gazebo in the day. Find the message and then get to Labelle as fast as possible. How much time did you say Milo was giving you?"

"Two days."

"Okay."

My cell phone rings. I turn it off and feel my face go red.

"Is that him?" Culler asks.

"Probably. Never mind about Milo, though." I clear my throat because I do *not* want to talk about Milo with Culler. "Thank you for doing this with me . . ."

"Thank you for letting me."

"You need it too."

"Yeah," he agrees. "I do."

"What was my father like with you?" I ask.

Culler is quiet for a long time, weighing the question. While he does that, I prepare to hear about a man I never knew, a man separate from my father. The one I want to know.

The one who would kill himself.

"Sometimes I want to ask you the same thing," he says, glancing at me. "What your father was like with you . . ."

"I asked you first."

"Well, he was kind," Culler says. "He was very kind, very passionate. Inspiring. But quiet . . . and when he was on to something he was really intense and you could tell he felt it—that he had an idea and he was going to turn it into something amazing—just by being near him."

"Topher said you were an art school reject," I say, and then I feel bad because those weren't Topher's exact words, but I'm too tired to think of a nicer way to say it. "I mean—"

"I thought I wanted something different then."

"Sorry."

"It's okay. I think it must've happened for a reason." He looks at me. "I thought it was over for me. I was really head fucked about it. But it brought me to your father and he made me feel like, for the first time I was doing something right . . . I always felt like the camera was what I needed to make sense of everything—to ask questions and then make answers out of the photographs I took. And then I felt—I feel so strongly—I have to share those questions and those answers. To me, that's art. He really understood."

"Are they posed?" I ask. "Your photographs."

He tenses. I feel it. It *is* too personal. I shouldn't have asked.

"They're truths," he says, which I guess is a vague way of saying yes and no. "But they're lies. Constructs." He looks at me for as long as he can before turning back to the road. "Eddie, I think . . . sometimes lies bring you to the truth . . . or help you reconcile with it . . ."

I roll up the window. The road moving under the car is hypnotic and I know I'm going to fall asleep. Don't fall asleep.

"Ever since he died, it's like it's gone," Culler says. "It's like . . . there's something between me and the photographs I want to take . . ."

I don't say anything. It's so sad. I wish my dad were here. Not just to be here, but because I wish he would answer for this. I want to make him answer for how sad this is.

"I want it back," Culler says after a while. "More than I can say."

My eyes drift shut.

E ddie, we're here."

My neck is stiff and my back aches. Here? We're here. Culler shakes my shoulder and says my name again. I open my eyes and rub my face and wait for the car to materialize around me. It's still dark out. The clock says it's three in the morning. Over six hours have passed and my eyes were closed that whole time.

"I'm so sorry," I mumble. Even in the dark, I can see how pale and tired he is. I wish he'd said something. If he'd said something, I would have stayed awake.

"It's okay," he says. "You were spent. Anyway, we're here."

And then I realize—here. Not just here in Valleyview, still moving and passing a WELCOME TO sign. But *here*. This is here: we're parked at the side of the road—a back road, by the look of it. Thick, healthy-looking trees line either side of it.

"Here," I repeat.

"Through those trees on my side"—he points—"I found the gazebo. It took me a while."

I'm awake now. I'm so awake.

"God." It's already happening. "But it's too dark to see . . ."

"I have a pair of flashlights in the back," he says. "Part of an emergency kit in case something happens on the road. I thought we could look now instead of tomorrow. We can look tomorrow, if we don't find anything tonight. But since we're pressed for time."

"Are you tired?" I ask.

"Yes," he admits. "But not for this."

We look at each other. We're doing this.

We open the car door and get out at the same time. I stretch, my bones crackling and popping, while Culler goes into the back for the flashlights. He turns one on, briefly illuminating his face, the bags under his eyes. He hands one to me and then he goes back into the car, grabs his camera, and gestures to me to follow him. We walk down the ditch. My footing isn't as steady as Culler's. He seems firm on his feet, already familiar with the place after walking it once. I slide beside him a little, almost fall, and he grabs me by the elbow.

"Careful," he says.

The weeds and the grass are ankle-deep and make my skin itch. It's buggy too, but these are small things, little nothings. All this inconvenience will reveal something great to me. I try to remember what the gazebo looked like in the photograph my father took, but for some reason I can't. I keep visualizing summer, something whole and complete. People there.

But when we step past more brush and through a clearing, Culler's flashlight glares over something much less whole.

"The water tower's just beyond it. You can barely see it."

I look behind me and I can't see the car anymore.

I turn back to the gazebo. We run our flashlights over it, slowly uncovering it. It's so much of a skeleton, it's hard to imagine what it must have looked like when it was new. The roof is all gaps, empty spaces where shingles used to be, and the trees seem to reach for those holes. The ground is swallowing it up. Grass creeps up the steps, the floor. I get dizzy—it's that same dizzy anticipation I felt when I was at the school.

"What if you'd never figured it out?" I ask Culler in a hushed voice, as we take the first steps inside of it. "This place won't be around forever. It's rotting away . . ."

I can't finish that thought. The idea of the last things my father had to say being lost to time—none of us ever knowing—is terrible.

Culler goes to the right, moving the flashlight slowly over the wood. I'm two steps to the left when my foot goes through the rotting floor.

"*Ow*, shit—" A jagged piece of wood digs into my anklebone. "God—"

"Fuck," Culler mutters. He waves the flashlight over my leg. He sets it down and tries to pull the wood back from my ankle with his fingers, but he can't. "Can you—"

"Yeah, it's just—"

"Easy . . ."

I pull my foot out slowly. The wood tears at my skin and by the time I've freed myself, I have a scrape and it's trickling a little blood. I wiggle my ankle around. It feels okay.

"Maybe we should come back in the day," Culler says uncertainly.

I shake my head. "No—we'll do this now."

"Eddie—"

"Seriously, it's fine."

He pauses and then goes back to his side of the gazebo and I go back to mine, waiting for the light to find me my father. It takes so long in the dark. Sometimes I get confused and end up combing through the same place twice. I feel bad for Culler, who must be aching and sore after all that time driving. I want to ask him if he stopped the car, even once, but I feel too guilty to.

After a while, he takes out his camera and takes some photographs, illuminating the whole gazebo with his flash, and for a little while, he becomes my light, and then we separate.

And then Culler says, "Found it."

Something about the way he says that makes me turn to ice. I stay where I am, staring at nothing, at the glow of the flashlight.

"It's okay," he says softly. "It's not bad."

I make my way over to him slowly. He steadies his flashlight and it takes a minute for my eyes to make out the deep grooves in the wood, and that thought of missing this to time, to weather, to ruin, crosses my mind again and makes me uneasy.

HERE I LOOK UP I SEE
S.R.

I press my fingers to the letters. I close my eyes. My blood feels hot, feels like it's burning itself through my veins. It's going to feel like this every time we find these. Intense.

"Find me," I murmur. "All these things gone cold and now I'm . . ."

Here I look up I see.

Culler doesn't say anything and I can't pinpoint the strange disappointment in my heart. I think I was expecting more. How am I always expecting more? This is so much more than I used to have. No, I wasn't expecting more.

I was expecting to understand.

"There are still two more places," I say.

Culler takes a photograph of the message.

"Two more," he repeats, and it's clear from his voice that, post-discovery, there is something unsatisfying about this one for him too. It's supposed to make *more* sense, not less.

I look up.

"Oh," I breathe.

"What?" Culler asks.

I point. He looks up. Through the skeletal gazebo roof are so many stars. So many. We're so far from the kind of light pollution that spoils the view, I think I'm seeing every star that is actually in the sky and I can almost convince myself they're coming down on me, and I wonder if that's what my dad meant by this one.

Here. Look up.

I see.

"It's beautiful," Culler whispers.

But how could my dad have known we'd find this place in the dark and see that? That anyone who found his last words would? I get another cold feeling in my stomach, something that tells me this is not what my father meant.

Or what if it was?

We go back to the car, and Culler shows me the photograph of the gazebo. The one my dad took. Even in the dim glow of the flashlight, my father's vision turned the gazebo a dark and unfriendly place, and the trees around it are sinister things. I feel heavy just looking at it. And I think, no, that's not what my father meant. It couldn't have been.

Because I can't convince myself the man who took this photograph looked up and ever really saw the stars.

Valleyview is smaller than Haverfield and bigger than Branford, but all of these places manage to look the same in certain ways. The people feel and look the same, like they've settled here even though they know there's something more—something better—just beyond where they are.

Small-town life.

Culler and I find a diner that's open twenty-four hours. We drink coffee and have eggs and bacon. I turn my phone back on and Milo calls immediately, but I don't answer and Culler says we can go straight to Labelle. It's only three hours away. The early traffic wouldn't be so bad. We could get there three hours on the nose. But I see how tired he is—his eyelids are drooping—and I suggest a motel.

"Not for the night," I add hastily, because even though we both knew this was coming, I'm sort of embarrassed about it now. "I mean—just for some of the morning. And you can sleep and recharge and I can take a shower . . . we can leave at like one and get there by four and then we can find the house . . ."

"Okay," Culler says. His voice is thick, exhausted. "That . . . yeah."

"You remember where the house is?"

"It took a while for your dad to find it . . . I remember where it is."

"Good."

We check into a little motel just outside of Valleyview. It's cheap but I guess you get what you pay for. I stand aside while Culler uses my money to pay for the room because I don't really want to deal with picking double or single beds and it's probably sad that whatever Culler picks, I'll go along with.

Also I want to see what he picks.

"Excuse me, miss?" The desk clerk asks. Culler and I turn. I point to myself and she nods. She's an elderly woman. "Can I have a word with you?"

I make my way over to her, looking back at Culler, who shrugs.

"Yes?" I ask politely.

She leans forward like she's going to tell me a secret. This close up, she's really creepy-looking, which just makes this whole place creepy by association. I have visions of *Psycho*.

Getting stabbed to death in the shower.

"Are you okay?" she asks.

I'm so confused about it. I have this really stupid moment where I think she knows my dad died. That suddenly, my grief is visible, radiating off me and telling the world I am a very, very sad girl. And then I realize she's looking very pointedly at Culler, and in this light, with his unshaven face, the bags under his eyes, he looks older than he is.

And I always look as young as I am.

"Oh!" I force a smile. And a laugh. "Yeah, it's fine. He's just my brother . . ."

"Oh," the woman says skeptically. "I see."

"But thank you." I try to sound gracious, like *thanks for caring*.

She nods again and I go back to Culler and I think I'm going to die laughing, which is a nice change of pace. He mouths, *what?* And I shake my head. When we get outside, I tell him what happened and he laughs about it, but not quite as hard as I do.

"Like, I think she thinks you're dangerous," I say. "Like you're kidnapping me or something. I think that's hilarious."

"Yeah," he says, but he's less amused.

"What?" I ask.

"Tired." He opens up the door to our room. I try not to get overwhelmed by the motel-ness of it. It's tidy and it's neat but I have the feeling this is the type of place that can never be *clean*. There are two beds and I'm not sure how I feel about that and before I can decide how I feel about it, Culler's saying, "I just wonder how much trouble I could get in for this."

"What do you mean?"

But I know what he means. I think.

He shakes his head.

"Forget it," he says. "It'd be worth it, anyway . . ."

I'm going to remember he said that forever. He flops down on the nearest bed, feet dangling over the side, and he's asleep within minutes. I brush my teeth and take a shower and change into some of the clothes I bought, but I'm awake. Totally awake.

I watch Culler for a long time. His chest rising and falling. I'm the age of consent. I think. It's not something I've thought about before. Does it matter if you choose to be in a car with someone? If they're just driving? If Milo decides to tell Beth that I'm not thinking straight since my dad died, and I can't make decisions, I wonder if she'll jump on that and have the police here in a second. And then all anyone will remember was that I "ran away" with a twenty-year-old student of my father's. My phone rings. I glance at Culler. He doesn't stir. I take the phone into the bathroom, closing the door behind me, and I answer it, but I don't say anything. Milo knows I'm there. All these minutes pass.

"Hi," I finally say.

"Hi," he says.

"We found another one," I say. "We're in Valleyview, but we'll be leaving soon."

"Beth told me you told her you weren't coming back."

I roll my eyes. "I just said that . . ."

"But I told her you would and she believes me."

"Okay."

"You are, aren't you?"

I don't say anything. That is unbelievably cruel of me to do, I know. But he knows I'm coming back and I don't want to say it. I just don't.

Because I've started to like pretending I'm not.

"I'm sorry we fought," I whisper. "Milo, you're my best friend . . ."

Neither of us says anything for a while. I pick at my nails and hear cars rushing down the highway through the tiny square window in the bathroom.

"I thought you were dead," he says.

"What?"

"When I found you." He pauses. "You were so still . . . I thought . . . I don't know. I thought you were both dead . . ."

I grip the phone tight, but I keep my mouth shut.

"If you come back," he says, "I'll tell you the rest."

"Milo, I'm coming back."

"I know. But I wish you wanted to, though."

I'm crying. I don't know when that happened. I brush the tears away and take a deep breath, and then I realize more tears are coming and I can't talk to him anymore.

"I have to go," I say, and I hang up.

run the messages over in my head, like what we've found so far makes it totally possible to anticipate what we're about to find next.

FIND ME
ALL OF THESE THINGS GONE COLD AND
NOW I'M HERE I LOOK UP I SEE

Culler and I don't talk much on the way to Labelle. Maybe there's no talking between me and Culler because I'm thinking of Milo. I can't stop thinking of Milo and our conversation and coming to the same conclusion over and over again: maybe I was the constant that faltered.

I don't know. It scares me if that's true.

I need to stop thinking.

I roll down my window all the way. Culler turns on the radio, cranking the volume so it can be heard over the wind. I close my eyes. Sight gone, my other senses heighten. The smell of the car. The sound of Culler breathing—maybe I'm imagining that, but I swear I hear it. I feel the car accelerate. We're going faster than we should.

The kind of speed that if we hit something, we would die.

Culler reaches over and presses his hand against my eyes. Just for a second. I keep my eyes closed and the only thing to do is take in the music, the sound around me. Every time I feel my mind drift back to the things that make me sad, I feel the music, the speed of the car, pull me back, like a temporary lifeline amidst all this other noise.

Eventually, the music stops, though.

Culler keeps driving and I listen to the road.

I open my eyes and he is looking at me in a way I can't describe.

We get to Labelle at around five, which makes us late because Culler takes a wrong turn and we have to double back. Labelle is smaller than Branford. That combined with Culler's memory means we find the abandoned house easily. At least we don't lose a lot of time.

It's in a rough-looking part of town. Every time I glimpse people wandering this street they all look sad, and I feel sad for them. I don't know why that makes me homesick, but it does. Culler can't get enough of photographing me walking it. He tries to explain it to me. He says something about the juxtaposition, how determined I look against this dying place, but I don't get it. But I love how passionate he sounds about it, I think.

"You sound like you're getting it back," I tell him, nodding at his camera.

His face turns a shy red.

The house is at the very end of the street and God, it's depressing. It could be the most depressing place yet. I studied the photograph my father took of it first and the photo is exactly what I'm seeing now, like he didn't have to try at all to bring the bleakness through.

He just took the shot.

It's sad when a place that has probably seen family, love, and death turns to nothing. It's rotting and worn. It looks like something bad happened to it that it just couldn't recover from.

It's . . . see-through, almost. Solid, but its guts are on display. The windows on the first floor are boarded up, the ones on the second are broken. The doors have been ripped away. We approach the house carefully, looking up and down the street. This is the most public place we've had to visit, and we don't want to get busted for trespassing or anything.

I keep thinking about what Culler said—I could get him in a lot of trouble, maybe.

We walk the overgrown path. Culler steps aside and I enter the house first. The floors are cheap wood, old weathered faces beneath our feet; something you'd cover with carpet, but the carpet is gone now, has been gone a long time. Ripped up.

Culler starts taking photographs. Of me.

He shadows me, at first, while I look around.

The hallway is a wreck. To the left, there are stairs. To the right, two rooms. Garbage litters the space, forming a trail to the back door—or the hole where the door used to be. Stained yellow wallpaper falls off the wall. Black mold—I think—edges down from the ceiling. I peer into the first room to the left. The kitchen. It's even worse off and there is no way we'll be able to get inside to look there. There's garbage everywhere. Random pieces of wood, lumber. Old plastic toys, which I can't quite figure out. The floors are linoleum, something seventies, I think. The counters and cupboards must have been white a long time ago, but they're completely stained and the doors are hanging off the hinges. The drawers have been taken out and thrown on the ground.

The living room is slightly less disastrous. It's littered with empty booze bottles, another space for people to come out here to hide and drink, and there's a couch next to the wall with a number of questionable stains all over it. There's a space next to it where a fireplace used to be. An old chandelier hangs from the ceiling by a thread. It smells terrible.

It's hard to breathe in here.

"Where do we start?" I ask Culler.

"You take the upstairs and I'll take the downstairs," he says.

"Okay."

He takes a photograph as I climb the rickety old stairs. I keep close to the wall. The banister doesn't look very stable.

Upstairs is somehow less derelict. The sun shines in through every broken window and I can hear kids playing down the street, outside. There's a bathroom, except there's a hole in the floor where the toilet used to be and the porcelain sink has been shattered. Two bedrooms. One has delicate-looking wallpaper, faded yellow, with white flowers on it. The other bedroom is all peeling paint, so much so that if I squint, it looks like the walls are melting. I'm wandering around that room and taking it in . . .

I'm not even really looking for it when I find it.

Was I a good daughter.

I remember the first time this thought slipped into my head. It was three days after, and Beth came over with all these pamphlets about coping that she'd gotten from God knows where— maybe she'd made them herself from information she'd gleaned from support Web sites—and one of them kept reemphasizing the importance of NOT BLAMING YOURSELF and it hadn't even oc- curred to me that maybe I should have been doing that until then.

Was I a good daughter.

Was I a bad daughter.

And then I decided he would have said if I was, he would have said that if he felt it, because it's not like he had anything left to lose by telling the truth.

And then I pushed all those thoughts straight out of my head. It wasn't me.

Except something about eliminating myself as a possibility made the question of why he killed himself worse somehow. And was I really sure it wasn't me? Five days after, I needed to know why. Why. Why. It was a thought-loop. Seven days after was my first visit to

Tarver's. The relief of not finding proof of myself as one of the reasons my father killed himself at that place was huge, even though I couldn't force myself onto the roof. Still, the question just got bigger.

Worse.

I'm sitting in a bedroom where the paint is peeling, my arms wrapped around myself. I wonder what happened in this place when it was new. Who lived here and what they did, and were they good people. Were they sad people. Are they dead now. Questions about things that don't matter, so I can push that other question out of my head: *was I a good daughter.*

It might have been me.

Imagine you're the weight around a person who jumps.

That you are what keeps them falling.

Culler sits across from me and he is holding my hands. I can't feel it. My stomach hurts. I think this is homesickness again. It's familiar. I remember when I was five. My very first sleepover. I thought I'd last the night, but I didn't. I called my parents in the middle of the night.

My dad picked me up.

"You wanted an answer," Culler says. I wonder how long we've been sitting here. "More than anything, Eddie. That's what you wanted."

THESE BURDENS
NOTHING WORTH
STAYING FOR
S.R.

Culler says I can't stay here in the house forever, but I think he's wrong. I could stay forever and wonder about being too much of one thing and not enough of another, but he won't let me. He makes me leave. He pulls me to my feet and walks me out of the house. I feel my body half-heartedly trying to direct myself back, but he won't let me.

I leave my voice in there, I think. My heart.

"You're making me nervous," Culler says. We're in the car and my head is against the window and my eyes are closed. "I wish you'd say something."

There is nothing to say. These burdens. Nothing worth staying for.

What could I even say.

We go to a motel on the other side of town, next to a public playground. LISSIE PARK MOTEL. It's so depressing. It's this small strip of rooms that faces the parking lot. And I bet a lot of them are homes. I bet some people live here always. Are they worse off than me?

Culler lets me into our room first. There's only one bed— something I should think about, maybe—and I curl up on it, bringing my knees to my chest while he moves around, taking off his shoes. Setting his camera down. After a while, he sits next to me and puts his hand on my legs.

"There's still one more place," he says.

But he sounds as uncertain about it as I feel.

I wake up after midnight.

Music thrums from one of the rooms down the strip. I roll onto my back and stare at the ceiling. A small sliver of light is above me, from a minute gap in the curtains, and Culler is next to me. I turn my face to him. His lips are parted. The way he breathes makes me feel something about him that I don't think there are words for.

I get out of bed quietly and lock myself in the bathroom, keeping the light off. I lean against the door and text Milo too many times, but he never replies. He must be sleeping too. The things I say to him are going to scare him when he wakes up, but I can't help myself, because it's what is in my heart and what is in my heart is killing me.

TODAY I FOUND OUT I'M A BURDEN.
& NOTHING WAS WORTH STAYING FOR.
IT'S BAD HERE.
BUT I THINK I MUST'VE KNOWN.
ONE MORE PLACE.
I WANT THIS TO BE OVER.

I WANT IT TO END.
I MISS YOU.
I'M SORRY.

I turn off my phone. I shower in the dark and let the water run over me slow and hot. It feels like suffocating and that almost feels like a distraction. Almost.

I cry.

I press my palms against my eyes and try not to be loud, but really I want to scream. I turn off the water and grab a towel, wrapping myself in it. I press my forehead against the door and then step back into the room and the light next to the bed is on. Culler is sitting up, awake. I don't say anything to him. He doesn't say anything to me. The carpet feels rough and dirty under my feet. I walk over to the window and look out. The station wagon is parked out front. There are people down the way, sitting on the curb. They look drunk and unhappy.

I move from the window and my eyes drift to Culler's camera in its case, open, staring up at me. I pick it up and raise it to my face. Blackness. The lens cap is still on.

I twist it off and look through it and I can feel Culler's eyes on me.

I turn to him and see him through the lens, a photograph waiting to happen.

Or it would be, if I could see it. But I can't. Nothing about his face, the place around us, changes. It's not art. It is still, unforgivably, the same. I wonder if my dad looked through his camera and saw the same nothing special I'm seeing right now.

Maybe that's what happened, why he killed himself.

Because how can you live with that, when you've known something so extraordinary?

But that wasn't it, was it, because if I know anything after today, it's this:

"It wasn't his art," I tell Culler. "It was everything else."

He holds his hand out.

"It was me," I say.

I hand him the camera and he turns it on me. He turns it on.

I don't say, *take a photograph,* and I don't say, *take a photograph of me like this,* but maybe it's understood.

The towel slides down until it's off, and I'm naked in front of him, and I've never been more exposed in front of someone else in my life, but it doesn't matter because I want to be.

"You *are* beautiful," Culler says, staring at me, as though this has only truly occurred to him now. He looks at me like I'm the only person in the world, like even he's an afterthought in this space. Like it's me and only me.

The soft sound of the shutter release. I wrap my arms around myself and my skin is cold, my hands are cold. I run my hands over my arms and try to imagine the way the light looks on my body. I take three steps toward Culler and I'm shaking. This is forever, these photographs. His taking them. For some reason I think of Beth and how old she is and how she'll always be old, and how she was probably never this young. I am so young.

I step between Culler's legs.

He lowers his camera and stares up at me.

"You trust me," he says quietly.

I nod, and then I lean forward and kiss him, bringing both of my hands to his face. He stays still and lets it happen, kisses me back. His lips are soft.

We separate slow.

He picks up the camera again.

Maybe one day, I'll decide I don't want to be here anymore, and this is what I will leave behind. Photographs. And whoever I leave behind can pore over them and try to make sense of it. Scratch their heads. *She was young and alive, untouchable. Why did she want to go?*

But they'll never make sense of it. Never . . .

wake up alone.

I know it before I open my eyes. At first, I think he's just stepped out and I imagine this whole moment where he comes back. Like a coffee run, maybe. And when I see him, my heart stops and then it starts again like it's beating just for him. I feel the space beside me in a way that knows he's been gone a while, and my chest is winding itself tight with everything that means for me. What does that mean for me. I don't move because I don't want to move. I keep my eyes closed because I don't want to open my eyes.

But eventually you have to move.

Eventually you have to open your eyes.

There's no note.

His things are gone.

I look out the window and his station wagon is gone.

It's just after lunch and that's when it hits me—how fucked I am and why did he do this to me and I'm fucked. I am totally fucked. I pace the motel, full of too many questions: *why did he do this to me, why would he do this to me, why did he go, where did he go, what about the church, why.* All the questions are so big, none of them eclipses the other enough for me to focus on one and work from there. Focus. Focus. Start with getting dressed.

I get dressed.

And then I end up over the toilet, sick to my stomach. Crying.

I don't know what I'm going to do.

What am I going to do. Unless—

Maybe he left a note with the desk clerk.

I wipe my mouth. Flush the toilet. I splash my face with water. I keep splashing my face with water until I can convince myself my eyes don't look puffy and red. I walk to the desk clerk's office. It's a man behind the desk, and the way he looks at me as I approach him makes my skin crawl.

"Did—uhm—" I clear my throat. "Did the guy I was—I came here with . . ."

And then I realize how it must sound to him already—how it makes too much sense with the way he's looking at me. And then I think I'm going to be sick again.

"He left," the man says. My stomach lurches, but I fight it. I am not going to puke in front of this guy over what Culler's done to me.

I don't even know what he's done to me.

Maybe he didn't do anything to me.

"Did he leave a note?"

"Nope." The man looks at me. "You have until three. If you're not leaving, you pay for another night."

"Oh," I say faintly. Another night. "Okay . . ."

I go back to my room and I get my wallet and then I go to the desk and pay for another night and then I go back to my room and sit on the floor and I comb through the place just in case I missed something. Something that says he's coming back. But there's nothing.

Why would he do this to me. We were supposed to leave today, for the church, and now I don't know what I'm going to do. The church.

The church.

I go back to the desk.

The man raises his eyebrows when he sees me.

"Uh, do you know where there's a church . . . around here?"

"Yeah. We got a few."

"I mean, an abandoned church?" I ask. "Somewhere around here? Maybe just outside of town . . . it's been there a while? It's abandoned."

He stares at me like I'm an idiot. "What do you need an abandoned church for?"

"Forget it," I mutter.

I go back to my room and sit on the floor again. I don't know what to do. I close my eyes and try to picture the church the way my father saw it, from the photograph. I remember the sky was ominous the day he took it, so it must have been going to storm, and the church complemented it perfectly. It looked angry.

And it's out there right now and my father is in it, and Culler has left me here without telling me how to get there.

And I don't know why.

I move from the floor to the bed. I fall asleep and then my phone buzzes on the nightstand, jolting me awake. Culler. I grab it. Milo.

Text message from Milo.

IF WE DON'T HEAR FROM YOU ASAP, CALLING THE PO-LICE.

I drop the phone. The shock of his message makes my hands go, or maybe they're just dying on me again. I pick the phone up and realize between this moment and last night, there are *a lot* of texts from Milo. I start with the first to get to the latest. CALLING THE POLICE. And then I think something stupid that doesn't even make sense, but that I almost believe: did the police come? Maybe the police came and took Culler quietly away in the night.

But that's not it.

He just left me.

BURDEN?
WHAT DO YOU MEAN, 'WORTH STAYING FOR'?
WHY IS IT BAD?
I MISS YOU
EDDIE WHERE ARE YOU
CALL ME
IF YOU CAN'T CALL, TXT

This morning:

I'M GOING TO BETH
I'LL GIVE YOU ANOTHER HOUR
EDDIE, CALL
JUST TOLD BETH. BETH TOLD YOUR MOM

Of course it all has to go wrong like this. It has to go wrong, just like this. I call him back, but the last thing I want to do is talk to him. I can't believe he went to Beth.

"God, Eddie—" This, before I can yell at him or tell him he's making everything ruined more ruined. He sounds so relieved, all my anger dies. "Where are you? Are you okay?"

I press my lips together, my throat too tight to speak. I curl the fingers of my free hand into a fist and press my fist against my forehead. I don't even know where to begin. But I can't not tell him. Culler left me and I have no way to get home.

"Will you pick me up?"

"What?"

"I'm in this town called Lissie. It's like fourteen hours south of Branford . . ." I realize how far that is for him to come for me, and how far it is to go back and all of a sudden, I just want to be *home*. I want this to be over. "Or I could take a bus, I don't know . . ."

"What happened?"

"Culler's gone."

"*What?*"

"He left. I'm at the Lissie Park Motel." I start crying. Stupid hot tears roll down my cheeks, and I brush them away and hope Milo can't hear them somehow. "And I don't know why he left, so don't ask . . ."

"What happened?"

"I don't know. We were going to the church. I woke up and he was gone."

"Do you think—" Milo sounds like he's struggling to keep a hold on, and something about hearing him lose it makes me feel slightly better. "Do you think something happened to him?"

"No."

But then I think, *maybe something happened to him.* But nothing happened to him. I know nothing happened to him. Just like I know my name. And my father is dead. And the sky is blue. Two plus two is four. Some things you just know.

"Okay, just—just a minute. I have to call your place and tell them. Or do you want to be the one—"

"No," I say quickly. Anything but that.

"I'm going to call you back in, like, ten minutes. Pick up when I do."

"Okay."

I hang up. I sit the phone in front of me.

I stare at it until it rings again.

"Eddie?" he asks.

"Yeah."

"Okay, I'm coming to get you," he says. "It'll be a while though. I won't get there until after midnight, probably. We'll crash and then head back . . ."

"They're letting *you* get me?"

He pauses. "I told them the only way you would agree to come back is if it was me."

"Is my mom okay?" I don't even really want to know.

"Beth . . . told her you ran away." He pauses. "I mean, that's what you did but . . . you know how Beth is. I don't know how she's doing.

I think she's freaking out." I don't say anything. He clears his throat. "You're going to be there when I get there, right?"

"Yes."

"Okay, I have to get ready and then I'll hit the road. I have my cell. I want you to call if there's anything."

"I'm room twelve," I say.

"Okay."

It's quiet. He's waiting for me to say it. I know I should say it. Simple: *thank you.* But I don't know how to say it. So I hang up because I know he'll understand.

I lay back on the bed, the shock of this all slowly settling, when I get an idea and it's so obvious, I don't know why I didn't think of it first. I sit up, grab my phone, and dial Culler's. It goes straight to his voicemail, so I hang up and call the apartment.

It rings and rings and rings.

"Hello?" It's Stella. And then I feel stupid. I know Culler's not there, couldn't have gotten there yet, but that's not the point. But I don't want her to know it's me calling either. "Hello?"

I bring my voice up an octave and hold the phone away from my mouth. Maybe she won't be able to figure it out. "Is Culler Evans there?"

"Oh—sorry, he's not," she says.

"Do you know when he'll be in? I have an extremely important message for him."

"Uh, actually he's out of town but I *just* heard from him and he'll be back later tonight. You can try him again tomorrow. Can your message wait until then?"

I bring the phone close and forget to disguise my voice.

"When did you hear from him?" I ask. "I mean, when did he call?"

"About an hour ago—I'm sorry, what did you say your name was?"

I hang up.

Fourteen hours gives you a lot of time to rationalize.

The more I think about it, the less sense it makes. Culler is not a fuck-and-run type guy. We didn't even have sex. He just took my picture. So maybe something happened, like a family emergency. The kind that's so bad, there's no time to tell anyone about it. You just have to get up and go and hope that the people you ditched will forgive you after you explain to them that it was a matter of life and death. That kind of thing.

I search the motel again, for a note, just in case. I check behind the bed where I find—ugh, an old, used condom. I search under the pillows and the mattress, feeling stupider by the second. The nightstand. I find a Bible there, like those motels in the movies, or maybe that's how motels really are. I check the chairs, behind the TV.

There's nothing.

I bury my face in my hands and think. Just think. This is not right. There is a reason he would do this to me.

Maybe—maybe . . .

Maybe he was scared of what we'd find at the church. My heart jolts at this—finally, an answer that seems feasible. Maybe it all got to be too much for him. I'd understand that.

It has to be something like that.

But I wish he'd told me he felt that way, because I'd forgive him that.

If he told me that, I'd forgive him.

How I wait for Milo:

I channel surf. I take four showers. I sit on the curb for a while and pretend Milo's just seconds away from pulling up until a gross-looking girl who might be in her early thirties comes up and asks me if I want to hang out in her room with her and her boyfriend. I go back to my room. I bury myself under the bed covers until I think of the condom I found behind the bed and then I take another shower. And then I decide it doesn't even matter, because I've already slept here. I climb back into bed with all of my clothes on and the TV on and I close my eyes and I go to sleep and the next time I open my eyes, it's late and someone's knocking on the door.

"Eddie? It's me."

I crawl out of bed faster than I can wake up. My mouth is dry and my head is heavy. I pad across the room and open the door and Milo stands there, trip-tired and pale, like he didn't even stop once, but when I glance at the clock on the TV channel guide, I know that must not be true. Before I can say a word, he wraps his arms around me and I think it's the best thing he could do because then

I can pretend I'm holding him up. Like he needs *me* right now and if I pretend this, I have to make myself forget about everything that's wrong and just be here for him. Keep it together for him.

What ends up happening is we both keep telling each other everything's okay.

I dig my fingers into his shirt.

When we finally manage to let each other go, the first thing Milo does is call home. He asks if I want to talk to anyone. I shake my head. I can't imagine talking to anyone there. Not Mom. Definitely not Beth. When I think of going home, I try to think of the place; my bed and the house. Things. Not the total mess of people that is waiting for me.

People who are probably really mad at me.

He goes into the bathroom to make that call. I don't know why. And then he takes a shower. When he comes out in a T-shirt and shorts, his hair wet and stuck to his head, his eyes drift over the lone bed in the room. He doesn't say anything.

"Do you want something to eat?" I ask awkwardly, after a second. "We can check . . . maybe something's open. . . ."

"I just want to sleep."

He doesn't look at me.

"Milo, I didn't . . ."

I gesture to the bed, feebly.

"Eddie," he says, "I didn't ask."

He crosses the room and digs into his coat pocket. He hands me a small envelope.

"What's this?" I ask.

"From Beth," he says.

"What?"

He shrugs. "Don't ask me."

"Not my mom?"

He pauses. "Your mom's been in her room since she found out."

I try to ignore the guilt that wants to take over. I open the envelope with shaking hands and find a little travel package of . . .

Vitamin C tablets. So Beth. But the note she's put with them is not so Beth. A folded piece of paper. Inside, her immaculate handwriting:

Just come home. We need you here. Beth

It scares me. It makes me want to cry, but I think I've cried enough today. Even I'm not stupid enough to overlook that *we*, because Beth chooses her words carefully. She wouldn't just put that if she didn't want to include herself. If she didn't want to include herself, she'd put something like, *your mother needs you here*. But she didn't write that. We.

We need you here.

This must be serious.

I put the note and the tablets in my bag. Milo lies on the bed, on top of the comforter. He lies on my side of the bed, not Culler's. It would be so weird if he was where Culler was. He throws his arm over his eyes. This silence—is so bad. It's a relief in a way, but it's bad too.

I turn off the lights and lay next to him.

I face the wall.

"What happened with Culler?"

"I woke up and he was gone."

It does not get easier to say.

"What happened before that?"

"Nothing."

I wonder how much I have to tell him. If I have to say the part where, no, we didn't have sex—don't worry about that, Milo—but he took photographs and I wasn't wearing any clothes. And then it feels like there's a weight on my chest because the last thing Culler did was *take my picture when I wasn't wearing any clothes*. No. No. No.

That is not the last time I'm going to see Culler.

I'll find him.

"Eddie," Milo says.

I go to the moment before that: the house. I tell Milo about the house and telling him is like being there again, seeing those words stuck in that place and saying those words out loud, they get stuck in my throat. What my father thought of this. Us.

"You scared the hell out of me," he says when I finish.

"Sorry."

"And you're no one's burden," he adds after a while.

We fall silent. It's amazing the way I am learning silence. My father's death changed the way I feel it, interpret it. It's this constantly evolving language I can't keep up with. A language I don't want to keep up with.

"Did you think I was going to kill myself?" I ask him.

"Eddie, don't."

"What would you have done if I had?" Why do I do this. Why can't I stop doing this. "What happened after you found me?"

I face him. I hear the same sad sounds coming from outside that I heard the night before. People staying up too late and being depressed on the curb.

Milo doesn't say anything for the longest time, but I know this time—he will.

"You were holding his hands," Milo says, and my breath catches in my throat because there really is no preparing for something like this, even when you know it's coming and you've wanted it forever. "You wouldn't let them go. They were locked . . . and I had to force each of your fingers from his . . . each one . . . and I made you let him go." He stops. "That's it. That's what happened."

"That's what you wouldn't tell me." I want to tell him that's not awful, that I was expecting worse. Or maybe there was a point before all this where it might have been bad, but everything that's happened since . . . it doesn't even measure up. "You should have told me."

He shakes his head. "You don't understand . . ."

I move closer to him. He seems to tense.

"Eddie, it's like you died that night," he whispers.

So that's it. I died.

I've been dead.

I blink back tears and pick at the mattress, but I don't say anything. I don't know what I could say to him. I don't know how to convince him I'm still here when I'm not even sure of it myself anymore.

When I wake up, I check my phone. Nothing from Culler. It's like he never existed. There is no evidence of him anywhere. But I know he exists, because I wouldn't be here if he didn't. I know he exists because every time I think of him, I want to break things.

Milo calls home and tells them we're on our way. I'm sick about going back again. I've barely been away, but everything's changed. Some small part of me wonders if Mom will wear this experience on her face, on top of Dad's death, and I won't be able to recognize her. Or if I will wear it on mine, and whether or not she'll be able to recognize me.

We pack up my things and put them in the car. Dawn has barely broken. Milo follows me to the clerk's office, where I return the room key. The clerk doesn't even look surprised at the addition of Milo, a different boy from the one I came here with.

"Thanks," he says.

"Have a good one," Milo says.

We're almost to the door when the clerk goes, "Oh! Hey. Wait. You're the one that asked about the church, aren't you?"

I turn. "Yes."

"Well, you ran off before I could tell you where it was," he says, and my heart stops. "You take Crispell Street and turn left onto Seals, keep going until you hit the highway. Turn right, first dirt road you see. About fifteen miles down, you'll find your absolution."

My stomach lurches. I turn to Milo, but he's not looking at me. I wipe my palms on my jeans. My heart is beating fast and insistent in my chest. I taste hope. I don't need Culler for this. *Ask him, ask him, ask him, ask him . . .*

"Milo," I say as we pull out of the parking lot. But I don't know how to ask so I just end up saying his name again: "Milo—"

"I know," he says. But that's all he says.

The church is plain and so, so neglected.

I don't understand why anyone would build it just to abandon it. It has echoes of a greatness it never achieved all around it. Like the person who built it wanted to evoke those cathedrals that are so fine and so incredible, they can't help but steal your breath away whether you're religious or not. But this church is a failure. Ramshackle and sad. It's tall. It almost looks taller than it should be or something, like whoever built it was trying to compensate, like height equals grandeur or something, but it doesn't. Not really.

I try to remember the photograph my father took of the church and try to forget that Culler has those photographs and now I wish I hadn't given them to him. I want them.

I remember the photo was ominous, which makes my guts twist up because I don't want it to be an indication of what we're about to find. The church looked angry.

Today, it looks as tired as I feel. All the staples of an abandoned place are here; what I'm used to seeing. Boarded-up or broken windows, peeling paint. I stare at it and feel all the hours and the road and Culler's leaving and Milo beside me, and I think no matter what I find here, this trip will have taken something important away from me.

Milo has to force the doors open with my help. The handles are all fucked up, so I have to hold one down while he shoves hard until we have access. We step inside. It's the mustiest, dustiest, oldest place yet. I don't know why they don't just tear it down. No one's using it.

No one wants it.

"Look at it," Milo says.

We stand there for a minute, silent. There's a choir loft above us. The door that leads to it is off the hinges and splintered apart. I keep looking up. The ceiling is ready to go. Spider-webbed stains spread out, like they're going to consume the place and the day they do is the day it will all collapse in on itself. What if today is that day.

The altar space is at the back, but there's nothing there anymore. Rows of short metal chairs, dusty and old, face it. I expected pews. Beside the altar is a door leading into another room. I bring my hand to the wall and run my fingers over it. It feels damp.

This doesn't really seem like a church.

"We'll find it and then we'll go," Milo says.

I point to the choir loft.

"I'm going up."

"Be careful."

I step through the door at the side, and climb the creaky, groaning, falling-apart steps—I have to skip over three of them—until I reach the top. It's worse up here. I don't understand how the place is sustaining itself. I imagine angels singing up here, praising God, and the floor collapsing beneath their feet. I run my hands over the ruined walls, half-heartedly searching for the last message. I look under things, shift garbage with my foot. It occurs to me I'm stalling. Part of me doesn't want to find it. I don't want to go back home and I don't want this to end.

I don't want it to end badly. I don't want it to be worse than what we found in the house.

I walk over to the railing and look down. I watch Milo move

along the wall, studying every inch of space on my behalf. He is intent, quiet, and I think about what he said.

It's like you died that night.

My gaze travels from Milo at the wall to the other side of the room and I catch sight of something that . . .

"Milo," I call.

He looks up. "Find it?"

"No." I point to the side of the room opposite him. "Were you over there yet?"

"Not yet."

He turns and looks and from his spot he notices the same thing I'm noticing. Intermittent footprints cutting a path through the dust, leading to the wall next to a window. Milo moves to it, but I say, "Wait," and he stops.

I run back down the steps, almost falling once, sliding into the wall to keep myself upright. I close my eyes briefly and just try to prepare myself for this, whatever it is. Little things are becoming clear: Culler was here. He must have been here.

But was he here before or after he stranded me?

And what if it's bad.

What if it is so bad, the only way to tell me is not to tell me.

The worst part of having no reason is that there could be any reason. I think of the message in the house. What if knowing is worse than not knowing.

No.

Not knowing is worse.

Milo stays where he is. I follow Culler's footprints to the far wall, where I see it, but it's not what it should be. The tell-tale initials of my father's are still there, scratched hard into the wood, *S.R.,* but whatever they gave weight to is gone.

Culler scratched the message my father left behind out—unless the last thing my father wanted the world to know is as abstract as a square space, purposefully worn away. But it's not. It can't be. I think. I don't know. I don't—

"Culler was here," I say. This is what I have decided: Culler was here. He did this. "I think he scratched the message out."

"*What?*" Milo asks. He makes his way over to me. "Why?"

Why. Why. Why. *Why.*

The question my life has become.

knew it," Milo says as we pass the YOU ARE NOW LEAVING LISSIE, WE HOPE YOU ENJOYED YOUR STAY! sign. "I knew he was just fucking with you—"

"We don't know anything," I say, but even I know how weak it is coming out of my mouth. I don't want to believe this. "Maybe he had a good reason—"

"We *know* he left you stranded in a fucking motel fourteen hours away from your home. What kind of reason would make that okay—"

"I don't *know*. Pull over."

"What?"

"Pull over," I repeat.

"Why?"

I unbuckle my seat belt. "Would you *pull over*?"

He finally pulls the car onto the shoulder and we roll to a halt. I push my door open, get half out of the car, and vomit all over the gravel and the pavement. I swallow once, twice, three times, pull my legs in, and close the door. I wipe my mouth on the back of my hand and lean my head against the seat.

"Okay?" he asks.

I nod, staring straight ahead.

He starts to drive again.

And then it starts to rain.

After a while, the sound of the rain falling against the car and the landscape blurring past the window suffocates me into sleep. Milo shakes my shoulder after I don't know how long. We're parked outside a gas station and it's not raining anymore.

"I have to fill up," Milo says. "I'll get some drinks, food. Break for a minute. I'll call your mom. Stretch your legs or get some air . . . or something."

He gets out of the car. As soon as I can't see him anymore, I get out my cell and call Culler. He must be there by now. It rings. It's a lonely sound. Pick up, pick up, *pick up*. And then, after thousands of rings—it feels like—someone picks up.

"Hello?" Topher.

"Is Culler there?"

"I don't know. Culler, are you here?"

And then I hear him. His voice in the background, asking, *who is it?*

And Topher says, "I think it's the lovesick high-schooler."

It's quiet for the longest time, then the muffled sound of someone putting their palm over the receiver. He's there and I want to scream into the mouth of my phone, *I know you're there. I know you're there. Why are you doing this to me. How could you do this to me.*

This kind of anger I've never known before. That I've gone from Seth Reeves's daughter who meant something, to this lovesick high-schooler in the span of like twenty-four hours is so unbelievably cruel.

"He doesn't want to talk to you," Topher says, and I hear Culler in the background again: *Topher, don't.* "Sorry, I mean, he's not here right now." He pauses. "But I'll tell him you called."

After he hangs up on me, I spend ten minutes in a sleazy gas station bathroom trying to keep it together. If I can get through the next ten minutes without crying, vomiting, or screaming myself hoarse, I can be in a car with Milo. But I don't know what to do about this humiliation, this hot, uncomfortable sensation all over me like the world can see this on me. I close my eyes and I count, trying to work it out. I count until ten minutes have gone by. I'm shaking, but not crying or sick or screaming.

I make a decision.

When I step out, Milo is leaning against the car.

"I want to stop at Haverfield," I tell him. "I want to see Culler."

Culler does not just get to do this to me.

When we finally reach Haverfield, it's dark.

I watch Milo drive. He's resigned to this. He doesn't want to do this, but he's going to do it for me. I'll never feel more guilty and less deserving in my life than I do in this moment, and I don't know why I can't just say that to him because he deserves that much. I think I don't say it because I'm too nervous to speak.

Haverfield's WELCOME sign sends me reeling. My head gets full of all the things I'm going to say to Culler, ask him. If he answers the door and lets me in. Talks to me.

This is so fucked up. No one changes this quickly. I don't understand how they could. And if he didn't, that means he was like this all along, but I don't accept that either.

I'm not that bad at reading people. I can't be.

I try to give Milo the directions to Culler's apartment, but I'm hazy on remembering or maybe I'm just tired or maybe part of my brain wants to sabotage me, so I don't have to do this. We circle street after street for ages, turn left, right, and when I'm about to give up—

There it is.

Milo parks across the road and turns the car off. I sit there for a minute that's not really a minute, but several minutes, twisting my hands. I want to ask him how to do this.

Because I don't know how to do this.

"Buzz up," Milo says. He gets my silence. "Say you have a delivery for Culler Evans."

"But it's night."

"They won't even think about it until after they've answered the door and it's too late."

"They'll recognize my voice."

"They won't recognize mine. Come on."

He gets out of the car. I have no choice but to follow him across the road and he asks me Culler's apartment number and he buzzes it and does the rest exactly how he said he would.

There's a delivery for Culler Evans.

The voice upstairs—Topher's—says he'll send him right down.

"Easy," Milo says.

I stare at the door, nervous.

"You have to go for this," I tell him.

"I'd love to stay," he says. "Punch him in the face."

"I don't need you to do that for me." I look at him. "Please, Milo."

"I'll circle the block." He steps off the curb and onto the road. "Ten minutes tops, Eddie. We should have been home by now."

I nod. Milo is getting into the car at the same time Culler opens the door.

When he sees me, he stops.

His eyes widen, his face pales.

And then before I can say anything, he's holding me.

And the worst part is—I want to hold him.

But I also want to slap him, hit him. Punch him. Tear out his throat.

I want him to tell me what he did to me was a mistake. Some horrible mix-up.

. . . After I'm done holding him back.

"What are you doing here?" he asks into my neck.

It breaks the moment. Ruins it. Brings me back to this awful reality. I push away from him—not hard. But it's difficult. There is still that part of me that wants to be near him.

I hate that part of myself. I want to be strong about this.

"You thought I wouldn't—" I break off. "You really thought I wouldn't want to know why you—why you left me there?"

"I'm sorry," he says. "Eddie, I'm—"

"Why did you leave me there?"

He doesn't say anything when I want him to be falling all over himself, trying to explain. He opens his mouth—closes it, like the words were there, but left before he could speak them. And then I remember this isn't just about the motel. Leaving me.

The church. What about the church. Everything.

"Were you scared?" I ask, and my voice is shattering already, hopeful, and I know tears aren't that far off but I refuse to cry in front of him. "Was that it? Was it about the church? You went to the church—" He flinches and I know I'm getting warmer. "You got rid of the message, didn't you? What did it say?"

"Eddie," he says.

"I mean, I was scared about the church too. It's okay—it's okay if you were scared."

But as soon as I say it, I hate myself for giving it to him. He's quiet. I wait. I want to shake an explanation out of him.

"You *left* me," I say.

"I was going to call you in a couple of weeks," he says with a feeble kind of urgency. I can't believe this is all he's giving me. "Eddie, I—"

"Why did you ruin the message? That was *mine*. It was more mine than yours—"

"I *was* scared," he chokes out. "Eddie—"

I cover my mouth with my hand. His words send a shock through me. That's what I wanted to hear. It's true. It's true. Didn't

I say I would forgive him that, if he was scared. But maybe not. Maybe I can't forgive him this. But maybe I should. And what does that mean, if he was scared? It was bad? Worse than what we found in the house?

"Was it bad?" I ask. He doesn't say anything. "It's bad, isn't it?"

He just stands there for the longest time. I wait and I wait and I can't stand it and I realize that's it: it just stops here. He won't say more. If Culler won't say more, I have to leave. I blink back tears. I'm not ready to leave. I can't. I didn't get what I came for.

I turn to look for Milo. He hasn't circled back yet.

"It doesn't matter," Culler finally says. "What was at the church."

I face him. "It's *all* that matters! It's the *only thing that matters.*" And he starts shaking his head and I can't believe this. "What's *wrong* with you? What did I—Culler, what did I do?"

"Eddie," he says, and the way it comes out of his mouth is too many things, it's familiar, almost comforting, and that makes me think, *no, Culler would never leave me stranded at a motel, fourteen hours away.* But it's sad, too. It's pitying me. "You didn't do anything . . . you . . ." He pauses. "You did everything but everything you did was right. . . ."

"I don't know what you mean. . . ."

Culler closes his eyes. They stay closed and he breathes slowly, like this is hard, but I don't understand. If he didn't want it to be hard, he shouldn't have left me at that motel. He opens his eyes.

"I felt something for you," he says. "And I got ahead of myself . . . I couldn't . . ."

"Culler—"

"Eddie, I put the messages there."

It's like—I can't breathe. There's no air. I step back from him. The words sink in and I decide—no. This is a joke. He's joking now. This is crazy and cruel, but it's a joke.

"I don't . . ."

"I'm sorry, Eddie," he says. "I'm—"

"You're lying—"

"I'm sorry. I'm sorry, I—"

And he keeps saying it, he won't stop saying it, and the more he says it the more I know it's true because people aren't just this sorry for nothing.

My face starts to crumple. What he says goes all through me and makes me numb. *He put the messages there.*

"Eddie, your father—"

"Stop it—don't talk about my father—"

"He was my . . . idol," he says, and his voice breaks. He rubs his face and steps back and from here, I can see he's shaking. "He was the only person who had any kind of belief in what I was doing and what I was trying to do. . . ."

"Stop it—stop talking—"

"And I'm so like you. I just wanted to know *why*—"

"Stop," I moan. "You lied to me."

"I couldn't work. I couldn't get past it. I couldn't get it out of my head—why he'd do that, but he didn't leave anything behind—but you know that." He sounds desperate now. He knows I'm shutting down. "I'd go to Tarver's all the time with my camera and try to figure it out and then I met you, and you were sneaking out there and I thought—she's like me—and the feeling got worse, because I know you needed to know too—"

"Don't . . ." I bring my hands to my eyes and all I can see is him, his camera. It's in my head. Everywhere. His stupid artist state-ment, what he said to me in the car: *sometimes lies bring you closer to the truth.* "Did you make it up just so you could *photograph* it?"

"*No*—not—I mean—"

I bury my face in my hands and he touches my arm and I jerk away.

"Don't touch me—"

"I told you—my work is questions, I can make answers out of art. And then I can let it go. Eddie, that's what I *do*. Except—I didn't know how to this time and then we went to the studio and you gave me those photographs—"

I shake my head. "I can't believe this—"

"And you were so upset because they didn't mean anything, and I thought, *I can give that to her. I can make them mean something*—and I thought I can work it out, I can make sense of it for myself with my camera, and I'll be okay and I can give you some kind of peace too. And I thought . . . I thought that's what Seth would have wanted. Or that he would understand—"

"Please stop, Culler—"

"But mostly because I felt something for you. I wanted to help you."

Milo says I died the night my father died, but he was wrong. I'm dying here, in front of Culler. I can feel my blood stop flowing in my veins, my heart slowing until it stops, and when I try to breathe, nothing happens. My lungs have given up. They don't want air.

"I thought I could give you an answer you could live with, but . . ." He swallows. "But it was just . . . lies. And you were so, so honest with me. In the motel, that night. And I couldn't lie to you anymore. I woke up. I panicked and I left." I am dead. I'm dead. "Eddie, I'm sorry—"

But I don't want to hear anymore. I turn and make my way off the curb. I don't know how I make my legs move me forward when all I want to do is sit in the middle of the road and wait for the first car to take me out. I'm already dead, see. It wouldn't make a difference.

"Eddie, wait—"

I stop. I don't know why I stop.

But I don't turn around.

I won't turn around.

"Tarver's," he starts, and I close my eyes and it's almost like he senses it, because he breaks off and waits and when I open my eyes again, he speaks: "His initials in the door there . . . that wasn't me. It was him."

I spot Milo's car making its way towards me. It sidles up to the curb and I cross the road and get in the passenger side and then I stop dying. I come alive. The worst kind of alive. My heart beating.

Blood raging through my veins. I'm breathing too hard, too fast. Milo stares at me, alarmed, but he doesn't ask. He won't ask. But I have to tell him.

I can't not tell him this.

"Culler lied," I say. "About everything. The messages. Everything."

"What?" He turns off the engine, grabs the door handle, and gets half out of the car before I grab him by the arm and pull him back in. "I'll fucking kill him—"

"Don't," I say, and he gives me this look, like out of all the sad people on the planet there are to feel sorry for, he feels sorriest for me. And my heart breaks again and again and again. Again.

"Eddie," he says.

"Please take me home," I whisper.

He starts the car.

Mom and Beth are standing on the front step when we pull up to the house.

Nothing makes me want to get out of the car less than that.

So I don't. I'm cemented to my seat and my throat is aching so bad. It hurts so bad. I can't move. They'll have to send for the Jaws of Life to get me out.

I'll grow old and die in this car.

Milo squeezes my shoulder.

"It'll be okay."

I shake my head. No it won't.

"They're not mad," he promises. "Just worried."

I shake my head again. I even cross my arms. A petulant baby pose, I know. But I'm not petulant. Not angry, not trying to be stubborn. I mean, I *am* angry, but it's not why I can't move.

I'm scared.

I am more scared than I can say.

I am scared to get out of this car.

It's easy for Milo. He's not scared. After he gets out of the car and after I get out of his car, he gets to go back to his home and not think about any of this and I want to ask him, *do you know how lucky you are to get a break from my life?* I would love a break from my life, but I have to stay in it, endlessly on play. The sun rises and sets, a day that never stops. So pause. I have to pause when I can. This is a pause. Stay in the car. Pause.

But they won't let me stay in the car, where life is suspended all around me. One of them—Mom or Beth—makes her way down the walk, to my side of the car, and opens the door.

I don't move. I don't look.

"Eddie."

My mom. But I stare straight ahead. I don't want to look at her. I don't want to look at her because she's a misery vortex and I'm already sad enough. If she sucks me into her grief, that will be it. This whole household will go under.

Even Beth won't be able to save us.

Mom reaches over and unbuckles my seat belt.

"Eddie," she repeats. "Honey . . ."

Something about the way she says my name this time makes me turn my head to her and nothing prepares me for what I see.

Her blond hair is brushed and pulled back into a loose ponytail. She is pale and drawn and her lips are red and flaky, eyes watery. But that's not the thing that's different.

She's dressed.

She's not wearing his housecoat.

This is the first time since the funeral I've seen her out of his housecoat.

I think I'm supposed to be happy about this. I think it's supposed to be a gesture, but for some reason, it levels me. I feel myself completely cave in, everything unwinding, all my parts breaking down. Culler lied to me. He lied. My father is dead. He killed himself and no one can tell me why. Why. And my mother isn't wearing his housecoat and I want her to be wearing his housecoat. I want to say, *don't give up on this,* because then I'm the only one left with it, but I can't speak. I lean forward so she can't see my face, and before I can stop myself, I start to cry. I cry so hard I can't breathe. I can't see. I feel like I'm coming apart.

Mom puts her left arm around my shoulder. Her right hand brushes my bangs from my face and she kisses the top of my head and she's saying, "Oh, Eddie. Oh my girl, my girl, my girl . . ."

sleep like I've spent a lifetime awake. I think maybe I have. I stay in my room for three days mostly, just trying not to think about anything. On the third day, Beth bursts in. She opens the curtains and light is everywhere. It hurts my eyes.

"Get dressed," she tells me. "Come on, Eddie."

I don't think she's a big fan of how Mom is dealing with my "running away." Mom's chosen not to punish me for my "act of grief." At least that's what Beth calls it when she tells Mom she should be punishing me for my act of grief.

"You cannot maintain this permissive state," I overheard her say. "We should have gone down to Lissie and brought her back ourselves. I don't know what you were thinking when you agreed to let Milo get her. This is how it starts. Total downward spiral."

"Thank you, Beth," Mom replied.

"What was in Lissie, anyway?" Beth asked sourly.

Nothing, I wanted to say. *Nothing was in Lissie.*

"Did you hear me?" Beth asks. "Up! Up! Up! It's summer vacation. I'm—I'm not letting you waste any more of it. *Up.*" She's trying to be back on form, but even I can tell it's different now. She doesn't sound as sure of herself when she says these things to me. She pulls my blankets back, leaving my legs exposed. I don't care. "Eddie, come on. Please."

I close my eyes. Beth never says *please* to me and means it.

"My father's dead," I say.

"Believe it or not, that's something that's never far from anyone's mind."

I open my eyes.

"Why is he dead? Why do you think he killed himself?"

The question startles her a little. She stutters—I actually make Beth stutter.

"I don't know. He didn't say and—and I—" She clears her throat and picks imaginary lint from one of my blankets. "I don't like to think about it."

"Why?"

"Because . . . I don't want to give up a second of this," she says, and I guess she's talking about living. "And that he could . . ." She shakes her head and blinks and her eyes get bright and her voice gets small. "It's a waste . . . it's just such a waste."

It's all a waste.

"Your mom wants you up and about. She's worried."

"That's funny."

"Downstairs, now."

"It's all I think about," I tell her.

She stares at me for a long while.

"You know," she says. "You're still alive. I don't know how many different ways I can try to tell you before it finally sinks in."

And she goes downstairs.

I stay in bed for a while longer.

And then I get up.

Mom is sitting at the kitchen table when I make my entrance. She's dressed.

This absence of housecoat shocks me. I wonder if I'll ever be used to it. She looks up when I enter the room and forces a smile at me, but the right side of her mouth twitches a little. She still looks like she's just seconds away from crying—I'm used to that. I hold on to that. I don't know why. It centers me from the fact that she's not wearing the housecoat. That she's in actual clothes. And she knows what I'm thinking all by the way I'm staring at her. She looks down at her outfit, self-conscious. She's in a lime green blouse and black jeans. It's something I've seen her in before, but she's not wearing it like she used to. She's lost weight.

"It looks all right, doesn't it?" she asks. I nod. She studies me and I'm not sure what to say to her, and then she pats the seat next to her and I sit down. Neither of us moves for a minute and then she gently tucks a strand of hair behind my ear. "I haven't been doing well. I'm not."

Like it needs saying.

"I know," I mumble.

"You're not doing well." She pulls me close and I let her. "And I want you to know that I understand why you left . . ." No, you don't. No, you don't. You don't. I close my eyes. She will never understand why I left. "And I want you to know things will change. Not overnight. I'm still trying to figure out where to start . . . But we'll get there. Okay?"

I don't understand this. I don't understand how she could be okay to start over without knowing why. That she's willing to try. How it's even possible.

"Okay."

I stare at the wall behind her head, where there is a photo of my father.

In the photo, he's laughing at us.

leave on my bike, pumping my legs hard because I'm angry and I don't know how else to work it out. Milo is at Fuller's right now and I need him. Mark is going to relieve him any minute and I want Milo to spend what's left of the day with me.

I bike across two streets and cut through an alleyway and round the corner off the main street. Fuller's comes into view. The place is busy. Two trucks and a car. I recognize one of the trucks. Roy Ackman's truck. It's taunting me, tempting me. *Let's go again. You call that last one a hit?* I speed up, pumping my legs hard, harder until I can feel it in my heart.

I just keep moving—

Until Roy Ackman rounds the side of it and I screech to a halt so hard I almost fly over the handlebars, but I don't. He stops, surprised, and then he smiles at me.

And laughs.

"Funny, Eddie," he says. He taps the side of his head. "That's funny."

He gets into the truck. He doesn't ask me how I'm doing. How my mom is doing. I want to shout after him. *My father is dead. He's dead.*

But I don't.

I throw my bike on the ground and I walk into Fuller's, where Missy, with her long, tanned, perfect legs, leans against the counter and talks to Milo. My heart goes into my throat a little bit, but when Milo sees me, he smiles warmly, like I'm the only person there is to see and that he wants to see, which keeps me where I am.

"Eddie," he says. "Hey."

Missy turns. "Hi, Eddie."

"Hi," I say.

"So I was just asking Milo if he wanted to waste an afternoon at Jenna's again," she says. Her voice is impossibly friendly. "Everyone's going to be there. You in?"

"No thanks . . ."

"Actually, I think I'll rain check it too, Miss," Milo says.

He's still looking at me.

"That's cool," she says. She straightens. "Okay, well. If you guys change your mind, you know where I'll be." She pats my shoulder on the way out. "I'll see you."

And then we go. Me and Milo. Together. Milo walks my bike for me. We go to the Ford River, where the water is still so painfully low and the grass next to it is still yellow and thirsty. I sit down and tilt my face toward the sun. Milo is next to me, stretched out. I can feel his eyes on me and there is so much between us that needs to be said.

"Thank you," I tell him. "For what you did for me."

I'll start there.

But the rest—I think it has to wait.

"You're my best friend," he says.

I bring my hand to his face. I run my fingers lightly across his skin. My index finger traces his lips.

I just want to feel that he's here.

I lay down next to him and rest my head on his chest. He

tenses just for a second, surprised, and then he relaxes and puts his arm around me. I don't want to talk. I just want to be quiet with him. Listen to his heart—that constant.

He kisses my forehead.

"What are you thinking?" he asks.

I think you could walk across the river and not get your feet wet. I think I've caused a shift. People are changing, slowly becoming different. I see the beginnings of it in them. I think I made it happen—or maybe it was just something that was always going to happen.

But I'm still the same.

A nd then the next thing happens, which I think is supposed to be the last thing.

I'm sitting in the living room, staring out the window when Mom comes in with a thick, padded envelope. She hands it to me. I look at her, confused.

"Package for you," she says. "I signed for it."

I stare at it for a minute, and then I notice the name on the return address.

Culler Evans

Mom notices it too.

"Oh . . ." she says, surprised. "Culler Evans . . . Culler Evans. Your father was teaching him. He thought he was just brilliant. He sent a very nice card after the funeral. Did you know him, Eddie?"

I look at her and she's looking at me funny.

"I met him once," I say.

She nods. I take the envelope upstairs to my bedroom. It's

heavy, a little. I sit on the bed with it forever, picking at the corner, before I finally gather the courage to open it.

It's hard to get my hands to work.

Photographs spill out onto the bed. So many photographs. A memory card. I'm not sure what to think as I sort through them. I'm looking for a note. I'm always and forever looking for a note, but there's none. Just photographs. Culler's photographs. Only his photographs.

I go through them slowly, my fingers trembling, and watch my life play out in stills.

First, Tarver's. Culler's empty interpretation of the outside of it. Photograph after photograph of this place, and I remember what he said. *Just knowing it inspired him; that he came here to be inspired . . . I'm hoping to feed off that.* And then, suddenly I'm there. This girl, peering into his station wagon. These photographs turn into my discovery of the initials on the door. I know this story; I lived it. The photographs he took of the studio after we cleared it out. The one snap he managed to get with me in it. These turn into the point-and-shoots he showed me at Chester's and those photographs turn into the schoolhouse. In one photo, I'm talking to Milo and I remember what we were talking about. Fighting.

We discover the second message.

The photograph of my hands after Milo left.

Then the photograph of the gazebo at night. The photographs of me on that street in Labelle. The house. Burdens. Burdens.

Nothing worth staying for.

The photographs in the motel. These give me pause. I stare at the girl in them and I don't believe I am her. Soft and naked. Porcelain skin, standing in front of Culler. The TV is a bright white light behind me and I'm looking at him in a way I am not sure I've ever looked at anyone before. My grief is on me. I can see it plainly in my eyes and that makes my throat tight and my stomach hurt. I remember how I felt that exact moment, knowing how alive and young I was—am—and I see it here, so much. It's like there's something there in me, just waiting to be realized.

And now it's gone. I think it must be gone.

I feel a deep sense of loss. More now, maybe, than before. I run my fingers over the pictures of myself slowly. I was so close. I thought I was so close. And now I am farther from where I started and everything is far from me because I still need an answer and I think of Culler and how far we are from each other, how brief and intense we were, and then over. It's amazing, when you think about it. And sad. Just like that. Like that—intense, everything, over.

Like being alive one moment and dead the next.

get out of bed as quietly as possible and then I open my window, fighting with it, because my hands are still dead. When it's open, I crawl out onto the roof, which slopes down, and make my way carefully to the very edge of it.

It's not a long drop, but it feels farther standing up, so I do.

I jump. I land hard on my knee, like the first time. I inhale sharply.

I'm bleeding, sticky red all down my leg.

But I'm alive.

Branford is so still this late at night. A dead town after nine o'clock. No cars headed anywhere, roads all silent. It's too far to walk.

But he walked.

I'll walk.

At Tarver's, the clouds cover the stars and the moon. I stand there, staring at the silhouette of the last place my father was alive, waiting for the clouds to part.

I wait. I wait. I wait.

Until I can see.

It happens slowly, the building revealing itself to me in the moonlight. I think I have been doing it all wrong, this whole time. I think to find some kind of understanding, you have to be as close to the truth as you can get to it. I walk up to the building and force the front door open. It takes all my strength and as soon as I step over the threshold I'm in the dark.

The door swings shut behind me.

My cell phone rings in my pocket. Milo. It's always Milo. I stand there and let it play out, let it stop, and then I text him.

FIND ME

I fumble through the darkness, holding my hands out. I know where the red door is. I know. I find it, my palm running over the wood. I try to feel out his initials. These ones are real.

These ones are true.

I pull the door open and move forward and—I'm already sick with it. My feet don't want to walk me farther than this spot, up the seven flights of stairs, until I get to the roof. This path my father carved out to his death. I press my hand against my mouth.

Seven floors. Seven floors up. I take the first step and my heart stops. I take my foot off and it starts again. I think that can't be good. I think something stupid: how could anyone climb seven flights of stairs with a dead heart. I put my foot on the first step and then the second. The third. The fourth step. Maybe ten steps and I'll start ticking again. Five. Six. Seven. Eight. Nine. Ten.

I listen for sounds of myself.

I'm still here.

But it goes slow, every step. My feet are too heavy and lifting them is almost impossible. I'm sweating by the time I get to the seventh floor, by the time I see the door that opens up onto the roof. That's when I hear the car.

Milo.

It took that long for me to get up here.

I stand in front of the door. I wonder if this is how Dad felt, nervous, excited. That he would finally leave everything behind. How long did he want to leave everything behind and who was he thinking of when he did this? His suicide is a question wrapped in a question in a question. But the answers must be here.

I step out onto the roof.

The air is bitter out here. I cross the roof, my heart beating hard in my chest. Would my father have walked faster, if we had gotten there in time? Would he have walked from me?

I walk to the very edge of the roof and climb up onto the ledge.

I'm just one step away when Milo comes out. I don't turn around. I just listen to his footsteps getting closer. I close my eyes and steel myself against a strange wave of vertigo. Legs shaking. I'm shaking.

It's a very long way down.

"I'm not going to jump," I say when his footsteps stop.

"You can't do this forever," Milo says.

But he's wrong. I could do this forever.

I know I could.

I can see the spot from here.

Where I found him.

"Tell me why he did it and I'll never come up here again."

"Eddie, I don't know," he says. "He didn't want to be here anymore."

"I don't know if I can live with that."

"I think you have to . . ."

"And if I don't?"

"Eddie, he's dead. Whether you do, or you don't."

I rub my hands together. I can't feel them at all.

I hold them out.

"They're still cold," I tell him.

He moves close to me and he takes my hands in his.

I step down.

He wraps his arms all around me.

"They won't always be," he says. "I promise."

We stay there until the stars disappear, one by one, and the sky slowly lightens. It's a new day and I know all I have to do is meet it with this thought in my head: there's an answer, a why, why he killed himself. And I can convince myself it's waiting for me, so far beyond what's in front of me now . . .

But I also know Milo is right—whether I do or I don't, my father is dead.

I hope he's found peace, wherever he is.

I hope I do too, wherever I end up.